The Accident

Books by David Plante

THE FAMILY

THE COUNTRY

THE WOODS

THE FOREIGNER

THE CATHOLIC

THE NATIVE

THE ACCIDENT

The Accident

David Plante

Ticknor & Fields NEW YORK 1991

Library of Congress Cataloging-in-Publication Data
Plante, David.
The accident / David Plante.
p. cm.
ISBN 0-395-56925-7
I. Title.
PS3566.L257A65 1991 90-22353
813'.54 — dc20 CIP

Printed in the United States of America

Book design by Robert Overholtzer

BP 10 9 8 7 6 5 4 3 2 1

What does it mean to say,
I pray for my heart to be purified?
I recall from my past religion
that purity of heart meant
to be free not only of sin,
but of oneself.
And how does one become
free of oneself?
By praying to what
is infinite?

The Accident

I

WALKING ALONG the Seine, close to the swiftly moving but heavy water that slithered against the quai, walking round the couples sitting at the edge with their arms about each other, one young man with his hand inside the unbuttoned blouse of the young woman and holding her breast, I longed for what I felt couldn't be fulfilled even by making love, only by throwing myself into the river, not to die, but to be taken somewhere else on its current, which, out at the center, streamed in smooth, shining, infolding waves.

God had made me, from my birth, want to be in another world. I had come to another, but this foreign world was not the one in which my longings could be realized. That was an altogether other world. The longings that pulled at me in Paris, because religious, were unrealizable in Paris, and I wished I had never believed in God.

I shouldn't have been thinking about God, but concentrating on the radiating circular grille about the base of the trunk of a plane tree, the green bench by the tree, and, behind the bench, the three small green women on a plinth facing away from one another and holding on their heads a dome from the inside of which fell, behind their backs, glistening water —

In Paris, I didn't go to Mass on Sunday. I knew I was committing a mortal sin, yet I had no guilt about that. I would have no guilt either, I knew, if I made love. I could go to confession to ask forgiveness of my sin of not going to Mass, and I in fact found out at a local church the hours of confession, but during those hours I went instead to the Luxembourg Gardens, and I did this in preference, and I knew, among the clipped hedges and the marble statues of nude men and women among the hedges, I had made the right choice. I had no doubts, and I felt the freedom of having made a choice and acted on it. But the longings I had, which seemed to have nothing to do with sin or no sin, I couldn't choose not to have.

Against those longings, I wanted, I wanted the small, intricate, graspable, and above all describable objects of this world: a window latch, a doorknob, the pull of a blind, a light switch, the porcelain handle for flushing a toilet, an electric bulb, a knife, a house key, a bus ticket.

But I didn't belong to this world, I belonged to God.

There were moments, walking about Paris, when I realized fully that I belonged to God, realized that my life wasn't mine but God's, and I would feel a slight thrill thoughout my body, and I'd sweat.

At those moments, details had a vividness that fascinated me, sometimes terrified me. I would see, in a street market stall, not an egg, not the straw adhering to the shell, but a thin seam in the straw.

I never hated God. Never. I never once thought He didn't have the right to possess me, and to oblige me to do His will because He possessed me. He was God, and His rights were unaccountable. But He hadn't done it, hadn't, and wouldn't ever possess me and make me His. I leaned against a building at the street corner — a black, water-stained stone wall that went straight down to the stone paving — and I felt the terrible thrill.

I was nineteen, the last year of my adolescence, the first year of my maturity.

I had been to Spain, and my longing was to go back to Spain.

II

I WENT farther north.

My reason for having come to Europe from America was to study at the Catholic University of Louvain, in Belgium, where, after the Spanish summer, it was my duty to go.

I took a train from Paris to Brussels, then a local from Brussels to Louvain. In the compartment, I sat across from a thin woman, also an American, going to Louvain. She was old enough to be a teacher, a very thin teacher. Her name was Pauline Flanagan. We were in the window seats, and I could see the eyes in her reflection looking at me when I looked out.

She had never been to Spain, and wasn't interested that I had.

Beyond her reflection, I saw low, flat fields bordered by canals and pollarded willow trees along the canals. The sky, as gray as the fields, was also low and flat.

"You'll like Louvain," she said.

Looking out at the passing fields, I said, "I've got to."

"That's reason enough to like a place," she said.

"I've got to study," I said, turning to her.

"Don't we all?" She laughed.

She wore big glasses, without frames, which magnified her eyes in her thin face. She looked like a teacher, but I imagined her, too, as a student, the skinny student she'd been at her high school in America, at dances having a good time joking with the guys and being treated as one of them. She had a good time even though the guys didn't ask her to dance.

Like a teacher, she asked me questions. Where was I from? From Providence. Did I come from one of those New England Catholic parishes? I came from a Franco-American parish. Pointing to herself, she said she was Irish-American.

I didn't want to talk about America, and I asked her what she was doing in Belgium. She was at the University of Louvain, writing a doctoral dissertation on culpability.

And then, as though she thought she was being too much like the teacher and should be more like a student with me, she said, waving a long hand, "Come on, what's the worst sin you've committed since you came to Europe?"

"A sin?"

"All right, you don't have to tell me. Tell me about a strange experience."

"I've been to Spain," I said.

"I've never been to Spain." She became a teacher again, and, after a moment, said to me, "So you're from a French Canadian parish in New England."

I admitted I was, yes.

The train stopped at a station, and I noticed a small palm tree in a garden, and I said, excited, "I didn't think I'd see one of those so far north."

Again Pauline became a student my age, and she said, "There are some pretty wild dives in Louvain, if you want some experience. People get so drunk they dance with chairs. Wild. Sunday morning, I often go to church with a hangover that makes the Mass a *real* agony —"

I looked out at the low, flat fields.

"Where are you going to be staying in Louvain?" Pauline asked.

"My first night, in a student hostel."

"Why don't you let me show you around some before you go to your hostel?"

When I pointed up to my big valise overhanging the rack above, she said it could be left at the *consigne* in the train station for a couple of hours.

She must have known I wanted experience, wanted to know everything there was to know about the world, all of it, every stone, brick, plank of it. I wanted to include, like a massively inspired *encyclopédiste,* everything.

At the *consigne,* Pauline spoke in Flemish to a man wearing a gray overall, who took my valise with a grunt.

Walking away, I said to her, "I'm going to learn Flemish."

As a teacher, she became irritated with me, the student. "You're not going to learn Flemish," she said. "You can't do everything."

I got irritated back. "I can," I said, but gently, so as not to show my irritation.

In Louvain, the light appeared to come from the stones, and in that stony light I saw stone faces shining out at me. The cobbled streets and squares had few people moving in them. The greater population of the town was the statues on its buildings, standing still in niches on façades, on the tops of gables, on the tops, too, of corbels and high turrets. They were inhabitants who, in their stillness, seemed to me to be waiting for something that would take a long time to occur. I looked at the face of a woman carved in a lintel to a doorway — just her face, so her body disappeared into the building — and she looked back with, I felt, the almost suppressed pain of her longing to have happen what they were all waiting for. Pauline and I walked among those stone people, some of them so densely populating the buildings they formed silent crowds.

We visited a church where there were no statues. It was all white inside, even its vaulted ceiling. The white pillars rose from a floor of black and white squares, on which were rows of low-seated, caned chairs that could also serve, when turned around, as kneelers. The bases of the pillars were simple square blocks.

Pauline said, "This is where you've got to come for Mass on Sunday."

I looked about the clear interior, and thought: But I won't come to Mass.

I left her to walk toward the altar, and heard from her footsteps on the floor that she was following me. At the altar rail, I knelt for her to see me bow my head and pray. When I stood, I turned to Pauline, who was calmly studying the altar, and I said, "I feel much better for that." I didn't. I knew I had prayed only for her to take me seriously.

Pauline didn't take me seriously, but smiled a crooked smile.

The organ started to play. I shut my eyes and I thought: I don't believe in God.

My eyes closed, it seemed to me spaces and spaces were opening up about me in my darkness.

Pauline walked slowly back down the central aisle, and I followed her out of the church.

She took me from one church to another. She showed me marble holy-water fonts, golden baptismal fonts studded with jewels, heavily carved wooden pulpits, more heavily carved wooden confessionals, paintings with sagging canvas in gilt frames, worn memorial slabs inserted into stone floors.

Out in the gloaming, she said, "There's one more place I want to show you."

I followed her through the darkening town to a park, a narrow park lined on both sides with trees that were dropping their leaves. Beyond the trees on one side was a long brick wall, and we stopped between two trees to look, over the wall, at a red and white brick tower with a conical roof of slates.

Pauline said, "I thought you might want to see this, given you're a French North American. It's the tower where Cornelius Jansen lived and thought up your religion."

I wanted to leave her, and told her I had to get to the hostel. She didn't stop me. I left her without asking how to get in touch with her.

That evening, I went out alone to walk around Louvain and tour it in the light of the streetlamps, and I was, I found, shy, as if all the shadowed statues were staring at me.

I passed a young man with pale white skin and black hair holding a girl around her waist, and when he looked at me I looked away quickly.

Around a corner, I saw Pauline coming toward me. She was with a man. She didn't stop, but called out as she went by, "Are you having a good time?"

"A great time," I called back. "A really great time."

"I'm sure you are," she said.

III

IN SPAIN, the totally Godless clarity had made me see shoes, burlap sacks, lemons on a white plate, as I had never seen anything before.

At the Catholic University of Louvain, the only person who had the patience to listen to me talk about Spain was a fellow American student named Tom Donlon.

We were in the same program, both from Jesuit colleges in the States, he from Fordham in New York and I from Boston College, and were spending our junior year abroad. One of the organizers in Louvain to whom we had to report when we arrived took the two of us — we hadn't met before — to see rooms so we could decide where we'd stay. Tom was plump. I was lean. All the rooms were just outside the ring road about the town, in the *banlieue,* but, as the town was small, within walking distance. The organizer, a young Jesuit in a soutane, told us about prices and said not to make up our minds right away but talk after and decide between us.

We walked along a *chaussée,* past a butcher shop where, outside, a small deer, its stomach split open and its ribs showing through the wound and blood coagulated about its muzzle, was hanging upside down. It was a warm October, the sunlight filled with diffusing dust. I had never seen an animal, a deer especially, hung upside down outside a butcher shop, its fur matted, its eyes staring at what it had seen as it died. But my great affectation was to assume, even when I was on my own, that I had seen everything, so when Tom, wincing as we passed the deer, said, "Look how horrible," I asked quickly, "What's horrible about it? They hunt them in the Ardennes."

"What's the Ardennes?" he asked.

I would never have asked about something I didn't know.

"Forests east of here."

He deferred. "Oh," he said.

We saw one room with dull yellow walls and brown linoleum on the floor and a single bed that sagged, next to it a nightstand, its door ajar and revealing a chamber pot. A crucifix was over the bed. The light, in a green glass shade, hung from the ceiling by a very long cord. This room was at the top of the house, the bare wooden stairs high and steep. The landlady — or, to call her what we later learned to call our landladies, using a Flemish word, the *bazin* — stood at the door, her hands clasped. She seemed to have palsy, as she shook a lot. Tom and I looked around the room, then asked the young Jesuit to explain that we'd let the *bazin* know. She shook so much it was difficult to understand if she was nodding agreement to this or not. She seemed frightened.

Tom said to her, in French he never learned well, *"Elle est une chambre belle."*

Tom was Irish-American.

She didn't smile, but seemed more frightened.

It was as if we were being as polite as possible but were an occupying force requisitioning rooms, and she had no choice but to accept what we decided. What we, or at least I, didn't realize was that she was frightened one of us wouldn't take the room, for it was late in the scholastic year, most students had already settled into rooms, and she needed to let this empty one for the money.

The Jesuit said someone would be back, definitely, to let her know, one way or another, what was decided.

I thought: Well, I'm not going to take that room.

We saw better rooms, each one, as the houses went a little farther into the *banlieue,* better than the last.

All the *bazins* appeared frightened as we looked.

The room farthest out, about a ten-minute walk from the first, was big, with a high ceiling and two French windows onto a balcony on the (European) first floor. It was papered, pale tan paper with a faint embossed design of diamonds and dots, and the furniture was huge: a double bed with a nightstand on each side, a double-doored armoire with oval mirrors, a dressing table between the windows with a big oval mirror, a wide table as a desk and shelves over it, and a great armchair before a coal stove inserted into a black marble mantel, which had an oval mirror hung over it. There was a crucifix above the high headboard of the bed, down which dangled an electric cord for turning on and off the lights on the wall. The *bazin* stood at the open door. She also shook.

A little thrill passed through me, a thrill that occurs when you're standing next to someone you want to make love with and you decide you must say something, and I said I'd take the room.

Tom said nothing, only continued to look around. Neither did the young Jesuit speak, but he looked at me hard. The *bazin,* blinking, shaking, seemed to be waiting for the Jesuit to approve of my decision.

I asked her how much the room cost. It was no more expensive than the others. I said I'd move in that afternoon.

Madame — in fact Mademoiselle, a more than middle-aged spinster with a long, soft white face and small, close-set eyes — looked at the Jesuit, and he said, not at all approving, that he approved.

He gave me a street map of the town and indicated with a cross where we were, and Madame, as I continued to call her, wrote out her name and the address on the blank back.

Outside, Tom said quietly that he'd take the first room we'd seen.

I felt embarrassed, and walked along with him and the Jesuit, but a little behind. The Jesuit was asking Tom questions, and he, in a voice that lilted a little at the sibilants, was answering them. I was left out.

The deer was gone from the butcher shop.

When we got to the house, facing the ring road but separated from it by high plane trees whose leaves were turning yellow, I said I'd go get my luggage from the hostel where we'd spent the first night and move into my room.

I thought: Someone had to have that room, why shouldn't I be that someone?

As I had very little money, I thought I couldn't take a taxi, so, sweating, I carried my two big bags back along the *chaussée*.

IV

UNPACKING, I found in the inner pocket at the side of my valise a missal, which I hadn't taken out since I'd placed it there when I'd packed, months before, in America. I held it, its cover black and embossed with Gothic arches and its pages marked with a thin red string that hung from the bottom edge, not knowing what to do with it.

I opened it, read, from *la messe pour les défunts*, "*. . . faites-les passer, Seigneur, de la mort à la vie . . . ,*" and shut it and put it in a drawer.

After I unpacked, I walked about in my room wondering what I should do next, as it seemed to me there was something else I had to do. The room was getting dim. I couldn't think of what I had to do, so said to myself, I'll go see Tom in his room. The sun had set, but the light outside, which seemed to have nothing to do with the sun, cast no shadows. I smelled coal smoke in the chilly air.

Tom opened his door wide, surprised to see me, and he smiled so his broad face became broader.

"Come in," he said. "I'm just finishing a letter to my mother and father."

Maybe that's what I should have done, written to my parents. I sat on the edge of Tom's sagging bed while he, round-shouldered at a table that served as a desk, wrote in the remaining light that came from the window.

"There," he said, and rose from his chair licking and sealing an envelope. "Now I don't have anything to do."

"I'm hungry," I said. "I thought we could go out to a café for something to eat."

"Let's go out and buy something and bring it back here to eat. That'd be fun."

The starkness of Tom's room would make it impossible, I thought, for anyone to have fun there. He lit the one light, the one with a green glass shade that hung from a long cord in the middle of the ceiling, and it hardly brightened the deepening dimness. But the brown linoleum shone.

"Back here?" I asked.

Tom looked at me as though he understood the place wasn't good enough for me.

"Fine, fine," I said quickly, my voice high. "That's fine."

At a grocery shop, I followed him from place to place as he searched for what he wanted, if he knew what he wanted. The small shop had an unpainted wooden floor. At the glass-fronted counter, with cheeses and cold meats under it, he, leaning low, examined the food, asking me as he pointed to each item, "Do you want sliced ham, or pâté, or a nice piece of cheese?"

"Anything, anything," I said.

A woman in a white smock stared at us from behind the counter.

Tom asked her, *"Que pensez-vous, Madame? Dois-je prendre le jambon, le pâté, ou un morceau de fromage?"*

The woman frowned. She shrugged and said it was up to him to choose whatever he wanted.

Tapping his head with a finger, Tom said, well, he'd take — he paused — the ham, two slices.

Thick slices? the woman asked.

Yes, nice thick slices.

She showed them to him on a sheet of white paper.

Tom said, "Ooou."

I took out my wallet, but Tom insisted on paying for the ham and the bottle of wine. He kept jutting out his elbow to push me aside as he took his wallet out and from it the money. Even after he had paid and he and I had put our wallets away, he continued to say to me, making that gesture as of shoving me aside, "No, no, I'm paying."

Over and over, he said *merci* to the woman, and *au revoir,* and *merci* again. I followed him out of the shop, Tom smiling from side to side as though he were walking through a crowd that was watching him pass, though the shop was empty. He carried the bottle of wine, wrapped in brown paper, in one hand, and the parcel of ham by the string with the other.

In a bakery shop, I bought bread. Tom, indulging me when I insisted, said, "All right, I'll let you buy the bread." He also let me carry the loaf.

In his room, I wondered why he had taken this one. We'd seen other, nicer rooms. Had he sensed that this *bazin* needed the money? In 1959, in American terms, the rent was very low, but she counted on it in Belgian terms. It occurred to me that he might have taken the room as a deliberate reaction to my having taken, without discussing it with him, the best — to show me up. But this was only to try to see the worst in Tom, to be as truthful about him as I thought I must be about everyone, myself too. Really, Tom had taken the room because it was the worst.

Its darkness and starkness indicated to me his lack of imagination, a lack of imagination all the more indicated by his believing in God — almost all the books on his one shelf were theological, and the one that leaned against the others to hold them up was a thick black book on holy orders — and also by his not finding it in any way imaginative that I didn't, which I told him as he was delicately unwrapping the bread from the brown paper and the ham from the waxed. When he moved, his clothes hardly did.

With one hand around the neck of the bottle of wine, he held the other out as if addressing a class. "Now, how are we going to uncork it?" he asked.

I was annoyed. I thought: He's making this *souper* all so complicated.

"Push the cork in with a pencil," I said.

"Oh, do you think so?"

"Give it to me," I said, and did it as he looked at me as if to remember, for the future, how it was done, not sure he'd be able to do it. Wine spurted out over the table.

While I sat at the table, he ran around the room for something to mop up the wine, and picked up a felt slipper.

I said, "Use the paper the bottle came wrapped in."

"What a good idea," he said.

He mopped up the wine I'd spilled, then didn't know what to do with the soaked paper.

"Put it in your chamber pot."

He did.

He asked me, "Will you use yours?"

I wasn't interested in chamber pots. I was interested in God. I said, "I haven't even thought about it."

"I was wondering about emptying it," he said.

He sat at the table across from me — the table that was also his desk when in a corner but that was now pulled out into the middle of the room under that low-hanging ceiling lamp, the bulb clear glass so the low-wattage filament inside was visible — and slowly poured out the wine.

After he took a sip, he made a movement with his shoulders as of ducking under something just a little too low for him to pass through erect, and asked, the glass held out, "You're an atheist, not an agnostic?"

I sat back. "I have no doubts," I said. "None."

"You're an atheist."

"Yes."

I told Tom that I thought a believer was unoriginal in his beliefs because those beliefs were all codified and received.

He pursed his lips, which made his chin almost disappear. "Why shouldn't they be codified by the Church and received by the faithful?" he asked.

I got up and walked up and down the small room while he sat at the table. "You can't have had much experience," I said.

"I've had some," he said. "I come from New York."

"You said the Bronx."

"Yes, but I went into Manhattan a lot." He smiled. "Once I went into Manhattan with some of the guys from Fordham, and we saw a prostitute in Times Square. Well, we thought she was a prostitute."

I smiled, though I didn't want to.

He said, "I guess you're right. I haven't had much experience."

I stopped before him and put my hand on my head and said, "Oh, Tom —"

He asked, "What's the matter?"

I said, "I don't know, I really don't know. I don't want to be here in Louvain. I won't be able to study. This morning, when we were being shown the university library by that Jesuit priest, I looked at all the books and thought, I won't be able to read even one of them, I know I won't." I dropped my arms, letting them hit my thighs.

"Where do you want to be?" he asked.

I sat down. I didn't want to tell him.

I poured out some wine and asked him, "Where did you go this summer?"

"To Rome," he answered.

"You went to the Vatican?"

"Oh yes."

"Wasn't that an experience for you?"

"To stand in Saint Peter's Square and feel embraced by the all-embracing arms of our Mother Church?" He raised his arms to form a circle and he smiled, a wide smile. "Yes, I guess it was an experience." He lowered his arms and smiled still. "Yes, it was an experience."

I asked him if he didn't have a vocation.

"Oh no," he said.

"It sounds it to me."

"I'm interested. I do a lot of reading about the holy orders. But I'm not up to it."

I looked away from him.

"Where did you go this summer?" he asked.

I said, "Spain."

V

I TOOK WALKS around Louvain, and often went into the narrow park where the trees became bare so I could see the tower of Cornelius Jansen through the branches. I knew little about his theology, except that it denied free will in men because of the greater, determining will of God, but if it was the theology of the original religion of my ancestors in the woods of North America, it was mine. I imagined him as a man withdrawn into darkness and staring at a skull. By instinct, I believed that nothing was possible, and this was a passionate instinct.

Sometimes, in the midst of misty hedges, I sat on a bench in that park, thinking of people who believed that they were doomed but for God's grace. They knew about impossibility, these people; they knew it was as impossible to pray to God to save them as it was to pray to God that they would never die.

My ancestors might have been shocked, and thought of me as no descendant of theirs, if they'd known I'd broken the one line that joined them to me. However much belief had evolved over the generations, they'd all had faith in some God, and I didn't. But when I thought about this, I felt no, they wouldn't be shocked, they'd accept my not having faith, because for them as for me there was no essential difference between having faith and not.

I hadn't, since I arrived in Louvain, written to my parents. I should have done this, and kept thinking I must do it, though I always sensed there was something else, even more important, I must do. All the while I was writing the letter I wondered what this something else was.

Chère Mère et cher Père,

Me voici! Your long-lost son is not dead, but alive!

By my letters, which I then sent to them regularly, my parents sensed something was wrong.

My mother wrote me this in a letter:

How I wish I could comfort you.

And for the first and only time, my father wrote a letter himself:

Cher enfant, nous avons eu l'impression de tes lettres que tu ne te trouves pas heureux là-bas où tu es, qu'est-ce que nous pouvons faire pour toi si loin? Nous prions à la divine Providence de te consoler et de te protéger, de te renforcir et de te donner la grâce de la lumière enfin de bien comprendre tes leçons, avec un coeur rempli d'amour et de bons voeux je prie que le Seigneur t'aime comme nous t'aimons.

Their letters meant little to me, but I saved them, so I must have thought they would mean something to me in the future. Or this: though I thought their letters didn't make any difference to me, thought them in fact banal, especially my father's, as I thought my relationship with them was also banal, I felt I had other relationships with them that weren't banal, and in terms of these other relationships their letters made all the difference to me. At my distance, it seemed to me that my parents were dead, and that the letters I received were letters from the dead.

I thought about their deaths: their being in an altogether other world, as different from this one as the forest from the town. They were deep in the forest.

I wrote to them not to worry about me.

I had a landlady who was taking care of me, I said. She lit my fire in the morning, and kept it alight when I was out, and left a scuttle of coal for me to keep it going when I was in.

Also, I had an American friend named Tom. He had, I said, because I knew it would reassure them, a background similar to mine in that his father was a factory worker. Then I was sure they'd like to know that he was a good Catholic, a much better Catholic than I was. He was a much better person than I was.

One day, walking along the sidewalk of square cement paving blocks to the center of town from the outskirts where I lived, I saw, ahead, a post at the curb edge, and I felt I had no control over myself and would bump into the pole, which appeared, in my helpless awareness of it, unavoidable. Attached to it was a yellow traffic sign.

I was aware of each fork with a bent tine, beaded glass of beer, frayed white napkin, little pressed-glass saltcellar, against the darkness that always shone round them.

Though I didn't believe in God, I could imagine Him as darkness. I could imagine Him as the darkness in which images occurred, the darkness that, when I shifted my attention from an image to what was around it, I saw as a state in itself, and that spread out in all directions beyond my sight. That vast darkness behind the image of a sunlit glass of water was the only way I could imagine God.

When images occurred to me, I found myself more and more glancing away from them into the space around them, and wondering what that space meant, and if the image could occur without it, and if it meant more than the image. And objects, too — stars, cabbages, leeks, insects, calves, serpents — were images in my apprehension of them, and were all surrounded by darkness.

Shifting my attention to that depth, I would imagine being drawn into it, head and shoulders and arms, chest and buttocks, cock and balls, legs, into the darkness that made everything that was human false, the darkness into which my ancestors, generation after generation, had died, and I loved that immense, encircling dark.

The God I was born to believe in, that God of my ancestors and my parents, was all unknowable in the darkness of His intentions, in which He held those who believed in Him with absolute authority. But I, I knew everything about God: I knew that He didn't exist.

My parents believed — I felt it in my blood — in that God. Believed? He was so vast, it didn't matter if He was believed in or not, because in His vastness there was nothing to believe.

I imagined myself leaning against an outside wall of a church at the edge of the forest and looking out. I imagined hearing axes in the forest.

I was unhappy in Louvain, and, during that autumn when I shaved at a little sink on a landing overlooking, through a large, many-paned window, a garden of cabbage stumps, lonelier than before in my life. I thought of going home, but I knew that in my immediate relationships with them, my parents wouldn't be the recourse I felt they would be in terms of those curious other relationships I had with them at a long distance.

I imagined myself leaning against the outside wall of the church near the forest, looking into the trees beyond the graveyard, praying for what is impossible, praying with the faith that the snow will not stop, that the mother will die, that the dead will never rise from the dead. Faith in the impossible was not different from no faith at all, but that was the faith I wanted.

I imagined myself going toward the woods, and as I did, the world revolved the trees away from me, so I'd never enter, but I wanted to. I wanted to go in deep where my ancestors were with the natives among the trees. The more the sphere of the world turned the woods away from me, the more I would walk, to see my ancestors and to kneel before them, pray to them for their forgiveness and their blessing. I knew their faith was great, as I knew my parents' faith was great.

Quand j'étais jeune, je priais à Dieu en français, la langue de ma réligion nord-américaine. Dieu, je croyais, ne pouvait pas comprendre anglais, la langue de ma vie quotidienne, la langue de mes jeux, mais ainque çe francais que parlaient M. le curé de sa chaire et les bonnes femmes dans le foyer de l'église. C'était nous, les paroissiens, les élus. À cette heure, j'entens une voix, qui vient de loin, dire, Dieu, Dieu, ayez pitié de nous, et encore plus loin de cette voix j'entends le bruit des haches dans la forêt.

VI

OUTSIDE in the streets of the university town I imagined I was inside, in a room filled with pieces of carved furniture. Before butcher shops, rabbits, small deer, and boar appeared to be laid out on heavy dining room tables or hung from the half-open doors of high cupboards in a dim room. Cracked pods and yellow chestnut leaves fell.

I sat next to Tom at a lecture. It was about how the ancients, watching the waves come in and out, in and out, wondered how something could change continuously and remain the same, inspiring in them metaphysical speculation. From time to time I glanced toward Tom. He was taking notes, his tongue between his teeth, his plump face low over the page of his notebook. As he flipped the page with a thick finger, he raised his head, looked to the side, past me, past the students in suede jackets and woolen scarves, and smiled. When I looked, too, to the side to see what person he was smiling at, I saw only faces intent on the lecture. Tom turned back to his notebook and wrote, and his constant smile made his cheeks bulge.

As we were going out of the hall, a student came toward us. Tom introduced me to Vincent Vosac, whom he said he knew from Fordham and who was also spending his junior year abroad. He'd come later than Tom and this was the first time they'd met in Louvain. Vincent was gaunt and dark, and Tom did not seem very friendly toward him, maybe because they hadn't been that friendly at Fordham.

We went out together to the courtyard, along one side of which were bicycles, and we stood for a while, talking. Students pushed their thin-wheeled bicycles past us. Pointing to one, Vincent said, "I'm going to get a *vélo,*" and I understood that what he was saying was that he knew the idiomatic word for bicycle. Tom asked, "What's that word?" I answered, though I had only just heard it, "*Vélo,* which means bike." "Oh," Tom said. I wanted Vincent to think I knew the word, that I knew all the words.

Vincent said, "I'm on the way to Alma's now," but remained standing with Tom and me, expecting us, or at least Tom, to ask what Alma's was.

I didn't ask, Tom did.

"The student café," Vincent said.

"You know where that is?" Tom asked.

I wanted to say where it was, but as I didn't know, I could only say to Tom, "How can you be here a week and not know where Alma's is? Everyone knows where Alma's is."

Tom shrugged.

I found out later that Vincent always appeared to want to do everything on his own, as now he appeared to want to go to the café on his own, but really he was waiting for one of us to say he'd like to go too, and Vincent, wincing a little for being made to do what he didn't want to do, would say, drawling, "All right, come with me." He liked to appear to prefer to be on his own, and never with Americans like us, and he always made us feel we were imposing ourselves on him, when in fact he needed us, or someone, to go anywhere, to do anything.

Vincent said to Tom, "I saw you looking at me during the lecture, and wondered if you wanted to tell me something."

"Was I looking at you during the lecture?" Tom asked.

"Right at me."

"Right at you?"

"Yes."

"If you say so, I must have been." Tom shifted his big body. He was waiting, I knew, for Vincent to ask him to come with him to Alma's. Tom licked his lips while waiting.

"Are you going anywhere?" Vincent asked.

"No, no." Tom opened his eyes wide, as if amazed that Vincent should think he was going anywhere.

"I guess you'd like to come to Alma's."

"Will you take me?"

Vincent winced so his black eyebrows met. "All right."

Tom asked me, "Would you like to come?"

"I'll come to Alma's, sure," I said.

The globed yellow lights inside the café showed through the steamed-up windows.

Vincent opened the door to lead us inside, and I sensed, in the way he went quickly to the nearest free table and sat and raised his hand and snapped his fingers and called *"Garçon"* to a passing waiter, that he'd never been there before. The *garçon* didn't come.

The three of us remained in silence until the *garçon* came. Pre-emptive, but half turned away, as if he weren't being pre-emptive at all, Vincent said, *"Un vin chaud."* The waiter didn't understand. Vincent turned further away and said in a louder voice, *"Un vin chaud."* I didn't know what a hot wine was. Neither did Tom, but whereas I wouldn't ask, Tom did. He said he'd have one too, said it to Vincent, who communicated this to the *garçon*. Leaning back in my chair to address him, I said to the *garçon* I'd have one too. Tom said to Vincent, "You've been in Louvain a shorter time than I have, and you know all the cafés to go to and just what to drink."

Our *vins chauds* were brought in steaming wine-glasses, too hot to touch. Vincent unwrapped a sugar cube taken from the bowl on the table and dropped it into his wine and stirred it with a spoon. I did the same to mine, and Tom did the same to his. Everyone else, I noticed, was drinking not *vin chaud* but tall glasses of beer, and I wondered where Vincent had heard about drinking hot wine.

When I lowered my lips to the rim of the glass, the vapors rose against my face, and this was a new experience.

Vincent, his eyes bright black in his pale, gaunt face, his short, stiff black hair sticking up on either side of a rigid part, kept glancing at people at other tables as if for someone he knew. He wore a black, high-collared sweater that hung away from his neck to reveal his sharp Adam's apple. He didn't talk to Tom or me, didn't even listen. Tom listened to me talk about Spain.

Suddenly standing, Vincent jostled the table and the wine sloshed in the glasses. I held my glass and saw, going for an empty table, a young woman, her blond hair looped loosely at the sides of her face, her lower lip thrust out in a pout, almost a scowl; she was angry, it seemed, at someone she had come to meet in the crowded, noisy, smoke-filled café, where the globed lights hung in the gray-brown air. Vincent called, "Karen," in an uncertain tone, maybe because he wasn't sure he recalled her name or wasn't sure she'd recall him, and called again.

As she came toward our table, Vincent said to us, "That's my girlfriend, Karen Larvens."

She didn't hear this. She pulled out a chair from the small, square table and sat, and said, as if she knew all of us, "God, I hate this place."

Vincent didn't introduce us.

"What place?" I asked.

Her pouting lower lip had a scar on it. She said, "Louvain," angry at me for not knowing what everyone should have known. "Because I'm a girl," she said, "I've got to stay at the girls' residence. I said my father gave me permission to get an apartment of my own, but they said they couldn't give me permission. So I've got to stay at Sedes Sapientiae. So I will. And am I going to give them trouble."

What was odd was that while she was speaking as forcefully as she did, Vincent kept looking around the café. Tom and I were attentive to her.

The soft flesh of her face appeared to sag just a little at her cheeks, and her long blond hair kept slipping from the pins that held it at the back of her head and sagged in tresses that fell down to her jaw, where it was pulled up under her ears. Strands hung loose.

"Why I came to Louvain to study, I don't know," she said. "As a punishment for being a Catholic, that's the only reason I can think of." The scar on her lower lip made her mouth a little crooked when she spoke. "I could have gone to some fancy liberal college in America — my father would have got me in — but I chose to come here, which is not liberal and in no way fancy. I wonder now if I'm taking my Catholicism so seriously, taking it on so much as a duty, to punish myself for being a Catholic."

I thought Tom would ask her what she meant, but he didn't, being attentive to her in such a way that he appeared not to hear what she said.

I asked, "Why should you want to punish yourself for being a Catholic?"

"Don't ask," she said, then, "Somebody order me a cognac, please, I need a cognac."

Attentive to that, Tom ordered it for her.

When it was put before her on the table, she noticed the glasses of *vin chaud* and said, "This isn't the season yet for those. They're for the winter. What are you doing drinking *vins chauds* now?"

His eyes shifting rapidly, Vincent looked about the café. Tom and I slouched in our chairs.

Singling me out, Karen asked, "Why did you come to Louvain?"

I laughed just because I was singled out. I said, "I think to get away from Catholicism."

She laughed, too. "That's a good one."

I was pleased I'd made her laugh.

Then, as if she'd only talked to me first to be able to talk to Tom second, she, leaning toward him so the loose strands of her hair floated, said to him, "You look as though you like it here."

Tom sat up. "I do."

Still leaning forward, "What's your name?" she asked.

"Tom."

She didn't ask me my name.

She said to Vincent, "I tried to get a message to you, or to your *bazin,* that I'd be late."

"That's all right," he said.

I thought: So maybe she is his girlfriend.

He stared at someone across the café.

Karen said to Tom, "You're the kind of person I should know here — someone who likes being here."

He raised his hands. They were broad, long-fingered, white. He said, "Well, you know, I'm not here for any amazingly new experiences."

Vincent said, "There's a Belgian student I know sitting over at that table."

"Then go talk to him," Karen said.

For a moment he sat biting the cuticle of his thumb, anxious about going alone to talk to someone, then he got up and walked among the chairs, pushing the empty ones against the tables, to a corner where a young man with a beard was drinking a beer.

Karen said, "I don't know about Vincent."

"What don't you know about him?" Tom asked.

"I don't know anything."

"We were at Fordham together."

"So you know about him."

"Not much."

"What do you know?"

"He's Polish."

"That's all?"

"That's about all." But in case Karen thought he meant something demeaning, Tom added, "Polish in the way I'm Irish."

"I could have guessed that about you."

Tom's plump Irish face blushed.

Karen said to me, "You're not Irish."

"No," I said, with a denial that meant no, I wouldn't ever be Irish, or Polish either. "I'm French."

"French?"

I nodded.

"I've never before met a French-American."

"There aren't many of us."

She didn't say what she was, and I felt she shouldn't be asked.

She drank the drop of cognac that remained in her glass, and after a moment she asked Tom, "What does your father do?"

He said, "He works in a factory."

She was ready to ask me the same question, but she wasn't interested enough, I thought, to ask, or she already knew just by glancing at me that my French father wouldn't be any more elevated in his working life than Tom's Irish father, or Vincent's Polish father.

Changing the subject, she said to Tom, "I'll bet you go to Mass every morning."

He giggled.

"Don't be coy about it," Karen said. "It's nothing you have to be coy about. If you're a Catholic, you're a Catholic, and going to Mass every morning is being Catholic and nothing you have to be coy about. I hate coyness. Which church do you go to?"

"I go to different churches," Tom said.

"When?"

"I like to go to very, very early Mass, when it's still dark out, so when you open the door to go in you see the sacristan lighting the candles on the altar, and no one else is in the church yet, not even the old women." He giggled again, couldn't help himself. "I guess I shouldn't like this, should like to be in the midst of a big congregation, all of us assisting at the Mass together —"

Karen said, "You're strange."

He pointed at himself and more than giggled, he laughed. "I? No, I'm not."

"Yes you are."

He shook his head.

"I hate going to Mass," Karen said. "I do go, but I hate it. If I went every morning, I'd do it only to suffer going to Mass. All I get out of fulfilling my duty by going to Mass on Sunday is to suffer my duty, and I hope the suffering will be for the remission of sins. I wish I could give up going. I'd be so happy if I could give up going."

"You shouldn't be going because it's a duty."

"Oh, I know that. You don't have to tell me that. But it's my only reason for going, and my only reason for being here at this university. I'm like my father, I guess. I know he sometimes wants to give up his company, wants not to have to go to Germany and France to run his foreign plants, wants not even to run his American plant, but he does it because he has to, because he considers it a duty to. I really, really wish I could give it all up."

It was as if Tom weren't really listening to her, but was more attentive to her than that.

She touched the top of her head along her part, then ran the tips of her fingers down her hair to the loose strands about her cheeks and pushed them back delicately, as though to expose her face to Tom.

He said, "I've got to get going."

Karen hardly said anything to him as he left.

She and I sat at either side of the table, she, her arms folded along the edge, studying her brandy glass. I felt, oddly, that we had had an argument, and that she now wanted to avoid confronting me. Perhaps I was guilty for the argument, and there was something I should say, though I certainly didn't know what. When she raised her head, her eyes were narrowed, and, her lashes fluttering, she looked across the room at Vincent and said, "Why did he ask me to meet him here?"

"I don't know," I said.

Her lashes still fluttering, she called out, "Vincent!"

She didn't have to call again. He left the bearded student and came back, and she asked him to order her another cognac. The three of us had cognacs.

Karen said to Vincent, "You knew Tom at Fordham."

"I didn't know him," Vincent said, "but I knew the stories that went around about him."

"Stories?"

"There was one about his going to a home run by nuns for spastics, to help feed them supper."

Karen laughed, a gutsy laugh, and said, "Oh God."

"There were stories about the jobs he took to try to pay his tuition, waiting on tables in a restaurant and stacking canned goods on shelves in a supermarket —"

Karen laughed that gutsy, vulgar laugh.

"I remember," Vincent said, "a story about his asking a girl from the school of nursing on a date to see a film in Manhattan, and his getting lost in the subway and her leaving him behind on the train to try to find his way from an old Chinese woman who couldn't speak English."

Again Karen laughed.

When, after we finished our cognacs, Vincent said he had to go and didn't explain where, Karen said to him, "Then you'd better go, and go fast." He sat for a while longer, biting his thumbnail and cuticle.

With a jerk, Vincent rose and went, and I sensed that

Karen felt abandoned. I knew I couldn't abandon her, but must wait for her to tell me she was leaving.

She said, "I'll get back to Sedes now."

"I'll walk you."

The stony streets had become misty, and the mist moved about people walking along the streets. Karen and I, side by side, walked among them.

She stopped at a shop window with mannequins in suede jackets, all standing rigidly in a row, facing forward, their eyes blank and their hair, men's and women's, painted on.

I sighed.

Karen turned to me quickly and asked, "What's the matter?"

I touched my forehead.

She frowned angrily. "Tell me."

"Nothing."

"Nothing?"

"No," I said.

She turned away from me to walk across the wide, sandy square with shops on all sides, their illuminated windows shining in the mist. I followed her, and we both looked in the windows, at shoes, chocolate cakes, books, babies' long lace christening gowns, black bunches of grapes in nests of white tissue paper, and bottles of wine lying packed with straw in wooden boxes.

We walked back across the square, on the far side of

which, near a bench, I saw Tom standing alone. The mist moved slowly about him. Karen saw him too, and stopped, as I did. Tom didn't see us.

When I stepped toward him, about to call his name, Karen put her hand on my arm and said, "Let him be."

VII

Each time Tom came to my room I had something different for *souper:* a meat pie, pickled herrings, a soft white cheese, cooked brains. At his *soupers,* he always had the same: bread, cheese, and luncheon meats. I wanted him to remark on my originality, and I wanted him to be envious of it. He never remarked on the food, as he never did on my room, where we sat at either side of the coal stove my *bazin* had stoked up for me, he in the armchair as my guest and I on my desk chair, eating off our laps.

His chin contracted and expanded as he chewed. He chewed his food for a long time, thinking, then swallowed only if it occurred to him to say something important, like "Oh, did you know all the Husserl papers are here at the university?" As I said I didn't and nothing more, that was the end of Husserl. Tom took another mouthful of food and chewed.

My primary reason for being with him — for wanting to be with him, because I would stand outside the house he lived in and shout up to his window more often than he would call me — was to remind him that nothing he was interested in could be in fact of any interest, and to make him jealous of what interested me.

I wished always I were somewhere else, perhaps farther away than Spain, where experiences would so overwhelm me I'd find it impossible to leave the place, ever. He knew this and knew I longed for that place and didn't really want to be with him except to impress him with my wanting to be somewhere else.

I would hit my head and say, "I can't concentrate, I can't."

He suggested that he teach me some Latin poems to help me in my concentration. After our silent *soupers* in my room, he'd take out his Latin text from his leather satchel with straps and open it on his knees and lean far forward then far back to get into the right position and open and close his lips a number of times as if to get them, too, into the right position, and ask me, in my distracted state, to repeat after him. All I can recall is *palida mores*. Tom wore black priest's shoes.

I thought he should be jealous of my atheism. I kept bringing it up. It wasn't agony I felt, I said, but a great happiness, a happiness I told Tom I doubted he could understand.

"You don't seem to be happy," he said.

"If not happy," I said, "something else greater than happiness."

Tom said, "You'll come back to God."

"No, I won't," I said, angry. "I won't."

"Then you won't," he said.

I was still angry. "That's like saying you'll be a little boy again, as if that were what every man should hope for, to be a little boy again. I know what it's like to be a little boy. I remember. It's totally sentimental to think that little boys are better than men. They're not. They're completely dependent on men, who tell them how to behave."

He said, "I guess you're telling me I'm a little boy."

"I'm talking about myself. Not you."

"I'm sorry then. One of my biggest faults is that I always think people are talking about me. Whatever anyone says, even if it's about the weather, I think is about me. I only ever think about myself."

I said, "You, think about yourself?"

"Oh, all the time," he said, "all the time."

"You never think about others?" I asked, as though that's what I myself always did.

He said, "Others? I'll tell you why I'm not up to being ordained into Mother Church. I'd be ordained only for spiritual reasons, reasons that had to do essentially with me. I believe the only valid reason for wanting ordination is to belong to an institution that will support you in doing good works for others, which reason has essentially to do with others, not yourself. I know that wouldn't be my reason. My reason would be only spiritual and have nothing to do with the world. It's simple."

I asked, "Come on, what good works do priests do, really?"

"People are comforted by them, you know," he said. "They are. They're comforted in their fear and guilt, and they're comforted at the hour of their death. I know that."

"And you couldn't do it?"

"I'm not good with people. My confessor at Fordham told me that."

"What do you want to do then?"

"As a lay person?"

"Yes."

"After I graduate from college, maybe I'll teach Latin."

"That would be something."

"I don't know where I'd teach."

"In a high school?"

"I don't think I could handle high school kids."

"You could do it in college."

"Maybe in college."

"But you're not sure."

"I'm not sure." He said, "I believe, like I believe nothing else, that the first responsibility of a person is to live in the world. I spoke to my confessor about this."

"I never had a confessor I could speak to."

"I'm sorry."

"What did he say?"

"He told me to get away for a while, to come here to Louvain, and think about what I can do."

"You have no idea what that could be?"

His eyes round and bright, he bit his lower lip as if he were about to say something he shouldn't, something wicked, then he smiled broadly. "No, no idea."

Before he left, he asked me, "I'd like to know if you use your *vase de nuit* or not."

I had to, I said, because the toilet was out in the back garden. But I emptied it myself.

He said, "I was emptying mine, too, because I was too embarrassed to leave it, but I was secretly emptying it into the sink on the landing early in the morning before anyone else in the house was awake. I thought it'd be all right. I didn't know the drain went right down into the *bazin*'s kitchen sink. Right into her dishpan. Poor thing, it's taken this long to tell me, she was that scared of offending me. She said, '*S'il vous plaît, monsieur, ne versez pas le vase de nuit dans le vaisseau.*' God, I was embarrassed. She insisted on taking it out herself after making the bed. So now I leave it. I guess I've gotten used to leaving it, as long as she's used to emptying it. But maybe you're right, maybe I should take it down to the outside toilet every morning. What do you think? Would I be doing the right thing taking it down myself, or should I leave it to her, as all the other students do? I wonder a lot about this."

VIII

Every morning, I had breakfast in my *bazin*'s dining room with three male students who had rooms farther up the narrow stairs of the house. They were Belgian. We had *tartines* spread with soft white cheese and sprinkled with sugar, and hot chocolate, and Madame my *bazin,* her head and hands shaking, stood to the side of the table and watched us eat. In a quiet voice she asked me questions which I answered while the students, who never asked me questions, listened. On dark mornings, the light that hung low over the table in a blue-and-white glass shade was lit.

"En Amerique —" Madame my *bazin* always started her questions.

I wasn't interested in America. I was far from America.

The students, whose heads were almost shaved up to their crowns, where the short hair was parted and combed flat, said, *"On dit qu'en Amerique —"* They didn't ask questions, but told me about America, or what they'd heard about America, which they held above my own experience of that country. If I disagreed — no, in America people didn't — they would repeat, that's what they'd heard.

After breakfast I'd go to meet Tom at his house, and we'd go to a lecture together.

I sat by him at the philosophy lectures, given by a priest in a small wooden amphitheater paneled in wood, the lectern in a box like a witness box in a courtroom, and I often wondered if there had been, at one time, a connection between law courts and lecture halls. Thoughts such as these went through my mind. I didn't take notes. Tom filled the pages of his copybook with notes. A lot of the lectures I simply didn't understand, for the French I'd learned in my Franco-American parish wasn't up to abstraction on that level. But the French seemed the kind Tom was most able to understand.

After a while I cut lectures, so when I did go I didn't understand the references to what had been explained previously.

As we were walking through the long, narrow, gray and brown park, past the round tower of red and white bricks and the round, pointed roof of slates, I said to Tom that I thought I'd give up going to lectures.

"I can help you catch up," he said.

I said, "I'm not sure I want to."

We walked to the end of the park in silence. I was now almost always silent with Tom. He seemed never to expect me to be anything but silent. However, just before we reached the iron gates out of the park, he stopped, and I did.

He raised an index finger to his jaw, and he said, pointing with the finger to a bench by a stone wall, "Come and sit with me."

I laughed. "Why?"

He had made up his mind. Tom was funny when he did. "Come," he said, and walked to the bench, and I, still laughing a little, followed.

"What do you want to tell me?" I asked.

His hands clasped in his lap, his ankles crossed, he asked, "What's wrong? Tell me."

"There's nothing wrong."

"You always say that."

"There's nothing wrong with me, then."

"So, what's wrong with Louvain?"

"There's nothing wrong with Louvain. It's just wrong for me at this time in my life."

"Where do you want to be? That's what you're thinking about all the time, isn't it? Where you really want to be."

"I wish you wouldn't try to act as a confessor to me."

"You can always tell me it's none of my business, and I'll never ask again."

That Tom didn't know how funny he was when he was being like a priest — which he would have been embarrassed to think I imagined him to be — made me not trust him exactly, but indulge him in his being like one, and I felt affectionate in indulging him.

"Ask me what you want to know," I said.

"I want to know what you're thinking."

I put my hands on my head. "I don't know, Tom."

"It's not about God?"

"No."

If I had imagined talking to anyone about Spain, this someone was very different from Tom, someone with experience, whose interest in me I wouldn't have to indulge, however affectionately, for being a little ridiculous.

Then I thought, Well, there's no one else, and a sudden great sense of loneliness circled us both on the bench. Mist was hovering in the bushes along the stone wall.

"Remembered moments come to me, and for some reason I find them unbearable. Why? Why?"

I felt that I was being not altogether unpretentious, but if there was no one else to know except Tom, this didn't matter, because Tom, not being the person of experience to whom I'd imagined talking, didn't matter.

"It happens all of a sudden that I find myself recalling

looking out a bus window at a group of women in long dirty skirts in a small dusty square, and one woman with torn earlobes because her earrings had been torn from them over and over, but she still wore the earrings, gold, pierced high up on her ears. Her cheeks had long welts of scars on them."

Tom sat with his head a little bowed, listening.

I stood.

"I have to be getting back to my room," I said.

Raising his head, Tom said quietly, "If you have to."

And I, as if he'd been forcing me to do something that I didn't want to do but that I finally gave in to, sat by him again.

I said, "I don't want these experiences to come back to me, but I'm also so possessive of them, I think they keep coming back to me out of possessiveness. I don't want to be possessive, but I am. I'm going to ruin my life out of possessiveness. Does this mean anything to you? You don't seem to know what possessiveness and jealousy are. I don't want to know, either, I don't. I hate those moments that come to me, I hate them."

Tom said, "I wish I could understand."

Mist was rolling down the long, narrow park to the gate. I said, "It doesn't matter."

"What about having lunch together?" Tom asked.

"All right," I said, laconically. I didn't want to go back to my room.

Above the wainscoting of the restaurant was a row of pitchers. Tom and I shared a pitcher of wine.

He said, "I don't think I'll ever forget the woman with the gold earrings."

Smiling, I said, "Oh."

Karen and Vincent came into the restaurant, and just when I was describing to Tom a rainstorm when the sun was still out and a bicyclist with a burlap sack over his head was pedaling through that illuminated downpour, he twiddled his fingers at Karen and Vincent, who came to our table. Tom asked them to join us, and I was angry at him for this and thought I was wasting my time telling him anything.

Tom looked at Karen as if he had been hoping to see her and his hope was now realized. Karen said to him, "Don't tell me, I know you're going to say not to forget my missal for Mass next time." When she said this, Tom glanced toward me and blushed, embarrassed that it was revealed that he and she had seen one another and he hadn't told me.

IX

One of the big reasons for not going to Tom's room was the cold. He never lit his coal fire. If he insisted on giving me a lesson in Latin there, I kept my scarf on. He wore two sweaters and a large, loose sweatshirt; the layers overlapped at his neck. The Latin grammar was on the table, and we, side by side, leaned over it. The pages reflected the dim overhead light.

I heard his name being called outside before he did, and sat back and told him someone was calling him. He, too, sat back to listen. A woman was calling, "Tom, Tom." He went to the window, opened it, and leaned out, and I heard him exclaim, "Oh, goodness." Excited, he found an envelope, put the key to the street door in it, sealed it by licking it, and flung it out the open window, then he rushed to the door to his room, opened it, and, pressed to the jamb as if an army were coming up and he were making room for them, he waited. Karen came in.

I looked around the room, as I imagined she would, then I fixed on a carafe of water and a glass on the mantel over the cold iron coal stove.

"It's freezing in here," Karen said.

"I know," Tom said, as if there were nothing to be done, ever, about the cold.

"Why don't you light your fire?"

Tom's cheeks shook a little. "Light my fire?"

She held up a paper bag. "I've brought some *souper*. But I can't stay in a room as cold as this. You'll have to light the fire."

"Then I'll light it," Tom said. "Now, let's see, to light it I need —"

"Don't you have what you need?"

He went to the door. His entire body shook. "I'll go get it all from the landlady." He bumped into the door on his way out.

I said to Karen, "He never lights his fire."

"Why?"

"As a small mortification."

"A mortification?" she almost shouted.

"Of the flesh."

"Oh," Karen said.

She sat, the bag on her knees, and we waited for Tom to come back. He was carrying sticks wrapped in newspaper and a black scuttle of coal, and he put down the makings of the fire by the stove.

I said, "I'll start the fire for you."

"Well," Tom said. "Well —"

Karen said, "Never mind. We don't need a fire. We'll go to a café. We'll have our *souper* there."

"If that's what you want," Tom said.

We sat in a corner by the window at Alma's. Tom smiled at the food Karen spread out in its waxed paper on the wooden table; smiled at the glasses of hot wine the waiter brought; smiled, as to express his gratitude more expansively, at the other students around tables, at the waiters hefting trays and serving the students hot wine and cognac and beer.

Tom stirred cube after cube of sugar into his hot wine, now seasonal. When he raised his eyes from his glass, I saw them fix on something behind Karen, who was sitting opposite him, and she turned to see what it was. Coming toward the table was a tramp in a long gray overcoat, babbling. He sat at the empty table next to us. He swung out his arm and knocked over beer glasses, which fell to the wooden floor and smashed. A waiter nearby put his tray down on the table and grabbed the drunken tramp's arm and pulled at it and shouted in hard Flemish; he got the tramp standing, and gave him a push. The tramp lurched and, bent over, cried out. Voices in the café dropped. The tramp, trying to keep himself standing, put his hands to his face and cried out again. I saw Karen quickly turn back to Tom, who continued to stare past her at the tramp. The waiter pushed him once more. He lowered his hands and, his upper body twisted, staggered to the door, which another waiter held open for him. The door was shut, and people began to talk again, quietly. Staring out, Tom smiled.

X

TOM GOT ME going to lectures again. Karen didn't come to these, and I didn't know which ones she did go to. Vincent came, but he sat separate from us in the lecture hall, almost every time next to a different student he had arrived with and would leave with.

I met Karen on a Saturday afternoon when, alone, I was standing in the square to the side of the cathedral, in the midst of the vendors' stalls, looking at stacks of slatted wooden crates with live chickens in them. She was, she said, searching for a big teapot for a tea party she was planning on giving in the reception room of the women's residence, and she thought she'd find one in a junk stall.

Searching for such things was a pleasure to me, and I said I'd help her. But she was the first to spot, in a stall among dented copper saucepans, exactly what she wanted: a teapot in the shape of a mansion with a hipped roof, the stones of the walls and the slates painted on, with a green door and windows with green shutters. The roof-cover was cracked, but glued. Karen clapped her hands and laughed that deep, vulgar laugh I'd heard before, which seemed to come from a much older woman, a woman who had had a lot of experience, and which I excused for being amusing, as the teapot was amusing.

The vendor tied the newspaper-wrapped bundle with cord in such a way that it could be carried by a handle. I carried it.

Karen said, "They're not going to like it at all at Sedes, my giving a tea party. But I'm doing it, I don't care. I'll tell them I'm doing it for my father. Let them try to stop me after that."

As we passed a *frites* stand behind the apse of the cathedral, Karen stopped and, studying it with fluttering eyelashes, said, "I shouldn't have any *frites*. I'm on a diet, and don't allow myself *frites*." A woman wearing a white apron inside the stand leaned out to hand a paper cone of fried potatoes to a man. Karen said to me, "Tell me I'm too fat and shouldn't have any *frites*."

I said, "I think you're not allowing yourself any because you feel you've got to deny yourself the pleasure, and for no other reason."

In fact, Karen needed to lose weight.

"You think so?" she asked me.

"Yes, I do."

She thought about this. "I guess I am like that," she said, "always denying myself small pleasures because I feel it's wrong to indulge in them." She stuck out her lower lip in an angry pout, then said, "Well, I'm tired of denying myself small pleasures just because I feel they're wrong. The time has come to break from all that." Her hands clenched and swinging, she strode to the *frites* stand. She did have a big bum.

The bundle at our feet, we stood hunched over our paper cones of hot, crisp potatoes and ate them with our fingers. Our breath steamed about us in the cold air.

Karen asked me, "Have you seen Tom?"

I knew this didn't imply that she hadn't seen him and was wondering how he was, but that she had seen him and wanted to talk about him.

"Not much," I answered.

Holding a *frite* up to her mouth, Karen said, "I feel Tom is in love with me." She ate the fried potato, chewing it and swallowing it quickly because it was hot.

A strange sensation occurred in me, something like a sensual stirring.

As I didn't speak, Karen, maybe thinking she'd said something that upset me, continued, "Not that I'd know for sure. Tom would never tell me. He'd feel he wasn't good enough for me, so wouldn't tell me."

"Then how do you know he's in love with you?" I asked.

"He pays me so much attention. He listens carefully to everything I say, and nods to let me know he's understanding my deepest meaning. I want to say, 'Oh, Tom, don't. What I have to say has so little meaning you're only being silly by paying such deep attention to it.' "

"I know," I said sadly.

"You know?"

"Yes."

She would tell me this to let me know she was closer to Tom than I was, not only because he confided in her and not in me, but because he was in love with her. I wanted to let her know that I was not at all interested in her or him, not at all, and yet something, which certainly had to do with them, moved in me.

Tilting her head to the side, she said in a soft voice, "I tell Tom he's too good, tell him he's goody-goody. For a while he just laughed, but finally he confided in me that he thinks that, too, about himself. He said he isn't real."

"Isn't real?"

"And he's worried about it. You may think Tom doesn't have any worries. He does."

"What does he think he should be to be more real?" I asked.

She laughed her hard, vulgar laugh. "Maybe more like me."

"What's that?"

"Someone who thinks no one is really good, never mind goody-goody." She crumpled up her paper and threw it into a waste can and brushed one hand against the other. "But even if he tried with all his might, Tom wouldn't be able to rise to the level of the weakest cynicism. He drives me crazy, he really drives me crazy. I keep telling him people are bad, bad-bad. He nods and says, with a sigh, 'Oh, I know.' He doesn't know. He can't know. He makes me want to be bad to him. Doesn't he do that to you?"

I laughed. "Yes."

"I sometimes think I'll try for a breakthrough, I'll do everything I can to get him to see that people are awful, just awful. The worst of Tom is that he agrees with you when you say that, he agrees to be agreeable, and sighs, and you know he doesn't believe it for a second, not one. Well, I'm going to make him see. I'm determined."

Only at the entrance of the women's residence, as I handed the newspaper-wrapped bundle to her, did Karen think of inviting me to her tea party in a week and a day, on Sunday afternoon.

On my way home in the dusk, I passed women washing the stoops and brick sidewalks before their houses, the steam from their buckets of hot water filling the streets.

I didn't mention the party to Tom, and he didn't to me, but I knew, by the way he insisted on asking me questions about Spain, that he thought I hadn't been invited, and he insisted on being interested in me to make up for that. I didn't answer his questions.

I said, "Spain seems so far, I feel it's impossible that I was ever there."

"Oh," he said.

But when I entered the reception room at Sedes — where, toward the back, there was a wooden table set with cups and plates of small cakes and the teapot — Tom, his hands held out and smiling, came toward me as if he'd been waiting for me.

He led me to a group of people standing to the side of the table, among them a tall, bald, fat man, whom he introduced to me: this was Karen's father. She was talking to Vincent.

Though I sensed that Tom, between us, expected Mr. Larvens and me to have a lot to say to each other, we didn't, and Mr. Larvens turned away to speak, in French with a loud American voice, to a young priest.

Tom said to me, "Mr. Larvens came all the way to Louvain from his plant in Germany for this party."

"That's nice," I said.

"It's a great party. You go say hello to Karen and Vincent, and in the meantime I'll pour you a cup of tea."

I didn't know if I should disturb Karen and Vincent, who were whispering. As I went toward them, Karen laughed out loud at something Vincent had told her, and looked at me with a look that put me at a long distance.

She said, "I invited the *maîtresse* of the residence to come to my party, but she hasn't come. She knew what would have happened if she hadn't given her permission. But she's showing her disapproval by not coming. Well, that's fine with me."

Vincent said, "What you should do after is make her a gift of the teapot."

Karen put her hand on his shoulder. "You're terrific," she said. "That's one of your best ideas. You're really terrific."

The saucer held by the tips of the fingers of both his hands, Tom came to me with a cup of tea.

"Would you pass around some cakes, Tom?" Karen asked him.

He went for a plate on the table.

Scrutinizing her little party, Karen frowned, and I saw in her face irritation that the people there didn't understand that this was a party of rebellion. She wanted to make people aware, and it really, really irritated her that people weren't, and that they didn't understand her rebelliousness. Vincent did. Maybe he was the only person who did.

She asked him, "What way can I present the teapot to the *maîtresse* that will most embarrass her?"

While he thought of an answer, Karen again scrutinized her party as if looking for a fight with someone there.

In corners of the reception room, in chairs about low tables, were residents of Sedes who had not been invited to the tea party.

Of the party, a Belgian student with a beard, the one I had seen Vincent talking to at Alma's, came to Karen, his big, yellowish teeth showing in a smile through his beard, and said to her, *"Dis-moi, Karen, tu ne peux pas parler à ton père à propos d'une position pour moi en Amerique?"* He wanted her to ask her father to get him a job in America.

She said to Vincent in English, which I presumed the Belgian student couldn't understand, "So that's why he wanted to be invited to my party."

"Why not?" Vincent asked.

Karen's hard laugh sometimes sounded like a cough. "Why not?" she repeated.

Tom was passing around a plate of cakes nearby, and Karen called him over to offer them to the student, whose name was Jacques, and to me and Vincent, too. She took one, the last one, and when Tom was about to go away with the empty plate she said to him, "Stay and talk with us." He continued to hold out the plate, which had a ring of blue roses on it.

"Tu veux que je parle à mon père maintenant?" Karen asked Jacques.

He raised his shoulders and jutted out his chin and

blew through his closed lips. This meant it was not up to him to tell her when to speak to her father.

"Pa," she called.

Her father turned toward her.

"Would you come here?"

The group around Karen made room for him, a big man.

Half smiling, Karen explained to him in French that Jacques, whom she indicated with a swinging gesture of her arm, wanted a job in America. She drawled. Was that possible? she asked.

It wasn't impossible, her father answered.

She said in English, still drawling her words, "I don't like him, but since he asked me to help him, and I can help, I feel I've got to. But give him the worst job going, because I think he shouldn't have asked me."

I saw Tom, staring at her, slowly lower the plate.

Karen's father laughed, and I understood where she got her laugh from.

Jacques, who didn't know what the laughter was about, was eating his cake. He could eat and smile at the same time.

His plump face pink, Tom said to Jacques, *"Monsieur Larvens, il rit parce que sa fille lui a raconté une blague."*

"Quelle blague?" Jacques asked.

Tom said it was a joke he couldn't translate.

Jacques wanted to know if Americans often told jokes.

Yes, Tom said, often, and at any time.

Could Tom tell him an American joke?

"Oh Lord," Tom said in English.

Everyone faced him as he tried to think of a joke.

"I can't," he said to Karen, appealing to her.

"Not to save your life?" she asked him.

All of us facing Tom laughed, even Jacques, who couldn't have understood.

"Try," Karen said.

"I can't."

"Come on, try."

Tom's pink face deepened to red and appeared to swell, so his collar was too tight for his neck. He asked, "In French?"

"It wouldn't be polite to Jacques to tell him a joke in English — he wouldn't be able to understand."

"I guess not," Tom said. His face seemed to become redder, to swell more. He said, looking at Jacques, *"Voici ma blague. Un homme aime une femme. Elle ne le sait pas, et il ne sait pas le dire. Un ami lui dit, Mais l'amour, l'amour vrai, ne peut pas être caché, et s'exprime lui-même, spontanément, d'une façon qui serait aussi une grande surprise. Un jour, la femme lui dit, Tu as un bouton sur le nez. Ah, il répond, ça c'est parce que je t'aime."*

No one laughed.

"It wasn't a good joke?" Tom asked.

Groaning, Karen said, "No."

Jacques looked puzzled.

Then Tom giggled.

Mr. Larvens said to Karen, "Are you going to come with me to dinner in Brussels this evening or not?"

"I haven't made up my mind yet."

Tom told Jacques, in case he might have doubts about going to America, that he'd have a good, a very good, time there: Americans were so friendly.

"Make up your mind," Karen's father said to her.

She said to him, "I left home to get away from people telling me what to do. I won't have it here, away from home. I'll make up my mind when I want."

Mr. Larvens suddenly asked Tom, "Will you come to dinner with me in Brussels tonight?"

Tom raised the plate and looked at Mr. Larvens as though he didn't know who he was and what he was asking him.

"If you go," Karen said to Tom, "I'll go too."

Vincent stepped back and began to bite his cuticles.

Tom turned to me.

"Tell him to come," Karen said to me.

"I'm not going to tell Tom what to do," I said.

"If you tell him to come," she insisted, "he will."

Vincent stepped farther back and turned and quickly left.

Tom remained facing me, and I realized that he didn't want to go, and because of that I said he should go, of course he should go. But, he said, he had work to do. I said he worked too much. That's why he was in Louvain, to work, to study. Don't, I told him, try to be such a goody-goody student. He lowered his eyes and after a moment said all right, he'd go. When he raised his eyes again to me I saw that, for the first time since I'd met him, he was angry.

Mr. Larvens said he'd be waiting later at his hotel for Karen and Tom, and he went to shake hands goodbye with the young priest.

Tom went to the table and put the plate on it, and stood there for a moment, then came back to Karen, who was now speaking with three of her other guests, three girls from the residence, and said he'd decided not to go to Brussels.

I was standing nearby and talking with Jacques, and I saw that Tom was surprised by Karen's leaning toward him and kissing him on the cheek. She laughed.

I left the party before Tom. That evening, after buying a meat pie and a bottle of wine, I went to his house with the intention of asking him if he'd like to come back to my room to have *souper* with me, but he wasn't in.

The next day, I didn't go to any lectures. I stayed in my room all morning. From time to time, my *bazin* came in to put more coal into the coal stove, though I told her each time that I could do it. After a slice of my meat pie and three glasses of wine, I, restless, went out.

Passing Alma's, I saw, close to the misted window down which condensation ran in rivulets, Tom and

Karen at a table. I could see them clearly only in the wide rivulets.

Karen was leaning toward Tom and talking to him, telling him something she had decided he should know for his own good, and he, his face set with a smile, listened.

About to go into the café and to their table, I saw Karen sit back and close her eyes and put her fingertips to her lids. I thought: She's crying. Now Tom leaned toward her and spoke, and she, her eyes still closed, listened, smearing her tears across her cheeks. With a heave of her shoulders, she cried more, wiping the tears with her palms. When she suddenly laughed, he laughed.

I entered the café and stood at their table. Smiling up at me, Tom appeared happy to see me. And so did Karen, who, her lids red and her eyelashes stuck together, asked me, in a voice made throaty by phlegm, to sit with them.

When Karen said, "My father's been insisting that I go with him for ten days to visit some of his Belgian business friends. They're the kind of people who amuse their guests by getting them to try on the ancestral armor. I've been, and I hate it. But my father isn't giving me any choice," I knew that this had nothing to do with what she'd told Tom while she was crying.

XI

I WAS GLAD Karen went away. Tom and I, just the two of us, had *souper* together each evening. Once we ate in his room, which I didn't like to go to not only because of the cold but because of the smell of overused laundry and unwashed body in the cold, closed-in air. All other evenings we ate in my room. As I knew Tom had less money than I did, I didn't mind sharing with him what I'd bought. I was glad Karen had gone because I wanted to be alone with Tom.

On Saturday evening we ate in a restaurant, then had *vins chauds* at Alma's.

Often I felt the urge to tell Tom I didn't like Karen.

He said to me, when I left him outside his house to walk on to mine, "Maybe we can get together tomorrow morning after Mass for coffee." I said, "Come to my room." Tom knew there was no point in asking me to go to Mass with him.

He appeared on Sunday morning with Pauline Flanagan and three sweet rolls. She was thinner than I recalled her, so her thin skin seemed to be stretched over the bones of her face. Her frameless glasses magnified her staring eyes enough to make them look as though they were outside the sockets.

Tom, I could tell, thought she was a character, and was excited by her. Also, he was excited to let me know he could make friends on his own with such a character. She sat in the armchair, and was so skinny that to lean back or to the side would have meant to sprawl; she sat upright, her roll on a paper napkin on her lap. Madame my *bazin,* showing them up, had asked me if she should make us coffee, and I'd said yes, please. I was sitting on my desk chair, my roll on my napkin on my lap. Tom insisted on sitting on the foot of the bed, his roll on a napkin on his lap. We were waiting for the coffee. Pauline said, "Hey, you guys, this is a treat." She was trying to convey that she was a regular guy, that we were all regular guys. Tom had met her coming out of church. She said to him in a stilted voice, "Did you listen to that God-awful sermon at Mass? I wouldn't blame you if you didn't. I listened, appalled, appalled by the reactionary tone against Mass in the vernacular. Did you listen? Jesus Christ, I sometimes wonder what I'm doing going to church to hear such sermons." This made Tom smile with pleasure, even giggle, and his face filled with the expression "Isn't she terrific?" To be a Catholic and say

Jesus Christ as she had was to be very much a regular guy. "I really do wonder," she said.

Madame knocked, though I had left the door open, and Pauline jumped up to take the tray from her, speaking in Flemish. They stood for a while, Pauline holding the glass tray with a chromium rim and handles, white cups and white coffeepot on it, talking. Madame smiled, then laughed, and left. Pauline put the tray down on my desk and poured out the coffee.

She and Tom talked about the changes in the Mass. They were both entirely for the changes.

I thought: This has nothing to do with me.

I had never had a feeling of kinship on meeting another Catholic. Perhaps, for all that it was called Roman, the Church I was brought up in was too French-American to be Roman. Pauline and Tom were as excited as if they were revolutionaries who had discovered each other, but revolutionaries who would always need the Church, and whose revolutionary ideas made them feel they belonged to the Church all the more than if they hadn't questioned Her. I couldn't at all understand their kinship in the Church as a worldly institution.

I had never, ever been able to belong willingly to any institution, but hated them all.

Pauline asked me, "What do you think?"

I laughed. "Nothing."

"What do you mean, nothing?"

I was embarrassed. Here I was at a Catholic institution of learning, but I was not a believer.

Tom said to Pauline, nodding, "He's an atheist."

I knew why he had said this: because it was sensational. The father of my freshman-year roommate at college, a professor of mathematics, was an atheist, my roommate had told me, and I, who for the first time had met someone who not only knew an atheist but was the son of one, would always say about my roommate, in admiration as well as for the real sensationalism of it, "His father's an atheist." And the sensationalism of my being an atheist reflected back on Tom, because he was nevertheless my friend. It was like saying: My closest friend is a communist, though I'm totally against communism. I was glad Tom had said it. He blushed red high on his cheeks and across his forehead.

"Are you?" Pauline asked me.

I raised my hands and laughed.

She said, "Hey, I'd like another cup of coffee if there's any going."

She and Tom continued to talk about the vernacular Mass, and what would be gained by it and what would be lost by no longer having the Mass in Latin. I sat back in my chair. Pauline checked at her watch and said, "Jesus Christ, I've got to go. There's this old *flamande* who lives in a damp little stone cottage on a canal in the Beguinage I visit every Sunday so I can speak Flemish with her. Poor thing, she probably thinks I'm doing it for her. Really, I'm doing it to learn better Flemish. She's taught me all the prayers in Flemish, so we pray together."

Pauline kissed Tom on a plump cheek when she said goodbye to him. She simply shook my hand and said she hoped she'd see me too. Her formality was not due to my being a nonbeliever; it was the way people almost always reacted to me. They reacted to Tom differently.

I heard Pauline talking in the entry with Madame, who'd obviously come out of her sitting room to speak a little more in Flemish. I shut the door to my room.

Tom was all apprehension, but he was trying to be even more enthusiastic than apprehensive. "Isn't she terrific?" he asked.

"I don't know."

Turned away from him, I heard him say quietly, "Oh."

"She was all right." I sat on my chair.

He sat again on the foot of the bed. "What didn't you like about her?"

"What does it matter?"

"I want to know."

"It should only matter to you that you think she's terrific."

"It does. But I want to know what you think. I thought you'd like her. Your opinion won't change mine."

Raising my voice, I said, to hurt him, "Well, she's not so interesting, is she?"

"Interesting?"

I slouched on my chair. "If you want to know, I found her really, really pretentious."

"Pretentious."

"She's like all believers. Their beliefs have to be pretensions —"

Tom's voice went as low as mine went high. "She's only trying to live her beliefs. What do you mean by pretentious? I don't understand. I'd really like to try to understand."

"You know what I mean."

"I don't. I really don't."

I got up and stoked the coal fire. I said, "Maybe it's pretentious even to have any beliefs at all."

Tom said, "I don't know if I'd go that far."

I had never allowed myself to express my jealousy of Karen's liking Tom more than me. My jealousy of Pauline's liking Tom more than me excited me to a degree that the excitement became a state in itself, and I could believe it had nothing to do with anything as personal as jealousy.

"People like Pauline," I said, "think they know everything about religion. But they don't. They try to make what they think convincing by, oh, saying they're not going to visit an old lady out of Christian selflessness but to get something out of it themselves, because everyone knows no one can be really selfless, so their selflessness would be totally unconvincing. I can't stand it. That's what I mean by being pretentious."

Tom blinked his eyes again and again.

"I mean, thinking about God and then acting, as convincingly as you can, on what you've thought out, so religion becomes all pretense, all acting out. And to be most convincing you've got to be a regular guy. Well, I hate regular guys. I'm not a regular guy, and don't want ever to have to pretend that I am. If people think I'm not a regular guy for not saying 'Hey' and 'Gee,' then that's fine with me, because I know I'm not pretending and that I would be if I said 'Hey' and 'Gee.' God, she was trying to convince us what a regular guy she was. Jesus Christ, Jesus Christ, she could swear like any regular guy. She was trying to convince us how human she was, even human enough to be culpable of swearing. She was trying to convince us she was the most human of believers. And that makes her totally uninteresting."

I was frightened of that sudden shift in my mind that occurred when I got excited and started it spinning on its own. As much as I insisted I must be free to think whatever I wanted, I was terrified of my mind's becoming uncontrollable. I needed a center of control.

As I walked up and down in front of Tom, he sat up straight on the foot of the bed.

"If religion were just human," I said, "a believer might just as well become a communist. Maybe that's what she and her kindred should become."

Tom continued to blink.

I wasn't screeching, not exactly, but as if I were screeching my voice was pitched to sound off the roof of my mouth. I pulled my hair. I said, "For a religion to be a religion it has to descend on you, descend and descend and descend on you, and knock you to the ground and make you totally helpless and possess you and make you believe whether you want to or not, so it's not you who decides if you believe, never, never you, but something that insists you're going to believe, you're going to believe, or die, or believe and die, something that you hate because it's going to kill you but that you can't stop. That's the only religion that is convincing. The only one."

Tom said, "Maybe you're right." Then he looked down and said, word by word, "I'd like to think that I had no choice, that God would knock me out with His love for me, which would be proof of His existence. Anyone would be right to want that. Still —" He rocked a little back and forth on the foot of the large bed. "I want, more, the choice of loving Him or not.

I'd rather believe that God was someone you could believe in or not."

"And you really do believe?"

He nodded his head. "And you don't," he said. "That was your choice."

I turned away from Tom. I sensed in our silence that I had hurt him, and I wondered why he didn't leave.

XII

I GOT UP and took the tray downstairs to my *bazin,* and thanked her. She asked me if she should put the cost on my bill. Yes, I said. Did I mind if she asked me if any milk and sugar were consumed? I wasn't sure, but she'd better add the cost of them to my bill. The milk pitcher looked full, however. Well, then, just the cost of the sugar. But could she serve the same milk to someone else? No, she must include the cost of the milk. What would she do with the milk? She had a cat, wouldn't the cat like the milk? She said that was very generous of me, but it was a shame to give my milk to the cat, which got all the milk it could want. I had an idea: couldn't she keep the milk until the next morning, and I'd have it for breakfast? She thought about this, her small, close-set eyes fixed on the pitcher, then said very well, that would do, though I could see that caused problems also, as she always bought so much milk and the milk she'd bought for breakfast would be left over, and what would she do with that? She asked me, did I mean to pay as well for the milk I would get in the morning? I said yes, of course. Well, she could use the extra milk to make a pudding.

I went back up to my room. Tom was walking about. I placed my chair at my desk and sat there, opened a book but couldn't read. Tom was keeping me from concentrating, keeping me from studying. I slammed the book shut and sighed, a long sigh, but he didn't interpret that as meaning I couldn't read because he was around.

He stopped behind my chair and leaned over my shoulder. "You're having trouble concentrating," he said.

"I'm trying to," I said.

"I understand."

I opened my book again, drew my chair closer to my desk and put my elbows on it, and said, "I've got to concentrate, I've got to."

All Tom took this to mean was that he should move more slowly. Not to disturb me, he reached very slowly past me to the shelf over my desk for a book, which slipped out of his delicate grasp and fell onto my book. I picked it up and, handing it to him, looked at him in the eyes. Tiptoeing, his shoulders hunched, he carried the book to the armchair, where he sat to read.

That he shouldn't realize he — he who assumed self-effacement to be a virtue — wasn't wanted made me angry. He never before had stayed more than an hour, an hour and a half, on his Sunday morning visits. Now he appeared to have settled in to read an entire book, a novel.

What does he want? I kept asking myself. And the more I asked myself, the more it seemed to me he must want.

Again I slammed my book and lifted it and dropped it on my desk, then I lowered my forehead to it.

Tom asked, "Are you all right?"

I rose and swung away from the desk. "No," I said, "I'm not all right. I'm never, ever all right."

He turned the novel down on his knee.

I realized he was staying for me. He'd thought I was in a state and he should be around. He might even have thought I wanted him to be around. This angered me more than if he'd stayed to annoy me, to make me feel I'd been wrong to condemn Pauline and, too, him, for of course he knew my condemnation was nothing more than jealousy.

Tom considered it a characteristic of his personality that he should always do the wrong thing and annoy people, but he never knew how to make up for annoying them — not just by leaving them, because that would have been a simple negative, but by doing something positive and complicated. I was interested in new experiences. He didn't know much about new experiences. I'd found Pauline totally uninteresting, and he supposed I also found him totally uninteresting. I didn't belong to the Church, had rejected it, so of course anything that had to do with the Church, even the vast ecumenical movement to change Her and make her more a part of the modern world, I'd find boring, and maybe resent. Hearing people talk about the Church with great concern I'd only find pretentious, as I'd find people talking with great concern about, say, ghosts. Tom had to think of some new experience, had himself to propose it, to get me, if not to forgive him, to see that he was trying, as my friend, to think of something I'd like to do, something that'd really interest me.

He sucked his cheeks in and puckered his lips to think.

Slowly, he closed the book, put it on the arm of his chair, and, pressing on the arms, raised first one haunch, then the other, stood, and, his lips still puckered, went to the window. Holding back one of the draperies a little, he looked out. He was, I guessed, pondering, revolving his tongue round and round his puckered lips and staring out through the net curtain that filmed the window. Then he nodded, turned to me, and raised a finger.

"I have an idea," he said.

He puckered his lips again.

I laughed.

With the kissing sound of closed lips suddenly parting, he opened his mouth wide and held it open so I could see his tongue, then he said, "Instead of having lunch in Louvain, we'll go to Brussels."

"For lunch?"

"Of course for lunch. I know a little restaurant there, and I'll invite you."

"I didn't know you've been to Brussels."

"I went a couple of weeks ago," he said, and in a throwaway tone, because he knew I wouldn't care but just to explain, "with a Church group."

"You didn't tell me."

"I'm sorry."

I was sure he'd in fact gone to Brussels with Karen and her father for dinner.

I didn't want to go anywhere with Tom. I wanted him to leave me. But I was aware that once I was on my own, I wouldn't know what to do with myself. I wouldn't be able to study. Again I was very behind in my studies, and though I knew the European students hardly studied until just before the oral exams, and hardly went to the lectures, but depended on outlines, in blurred carbon copies, of the lectures that someone at some point had compiled from notes and that were passed around, I wasn't used to this, and felt I wouldn't be able to make up what the Belgian students would be able to in a month. Even without the presence of Tom, I wouldn't be able to concentrate.

Whenever, alone, I did try to read, I'd keep looking

through the print at something below the level of the words on the page, some utter blankness, and I'd close the book and wonder what I should do. I'd usually end up masturbating, after which I'd go into a worse state of not knowing what to do, a worse state of not being able to concentrate.

I never talked about sex with Tom. It would have disgusted me to do that, as if talking about sex with him implied having it with him in some form, and this repelled me. If Tom had a sex, I wanted to think mine was completely different, and I tolerated his only by his never referring to it. All he'd once said about sex to me was that he'd read the poems of a man who, despite his desperate efforts, kept giving in to the sin of sexual impurity, with himself and others, after which he'd write poems, imploring prayers rather than poems, to the Virgin Mother in Her purity to help him remain pure. Tom had said they were very beautiful poems. I didn't ask who the poet was.

I wanted to say to Tom that I didn't feel like going to Brussels, and that really, I had to do some reading and, more than that, try to remember what I'd read.

Tom was intelligent. He could read a book quickly, remember it all, and discuss it. I couldn't ever discuss a book.

I found it difficult to say no to Tom. To say no required all my intention to hurt him, and though I did this often enough I knew it was wrong of me. Most often, I'd half say no, so he thought I could almost never make up my mind what I wanted to do. Well, that was true about what others suggested to me. I was stubborn, and only ever wanted to do what I wanted to do, and it seemed to me a defeat to agree to do what someone else wanted to do. If I'd said to Tom, "Let's go to Brussels," he would have responded, "That's a good idea, you've always got good ideas," but I couldn't respond to Tom in that way. The final reason for saying well, all right, was Sunday in Louvain.

The streets and squares of the small Belgian university town, which was also a center for the brewing of beer, became on Sunday like the corridors and rooms of a house filled with statues. I had walked up and down the streets and in and out of the squares, on my own or with Tom, but alone or with Tom I always went back to my room afterward with the sense of great emptiness, however much I had yearned for something to happen. Attention to that architectural detail, that cat on a stoop, those books in a bookshop window, those hanging rosaries and crucifix with the arms of the Corpus raised almost in a circle in another shop window — strained attention to these objects should have made something happen, but it didn't, and instead my attention seemed defeated by them because they were not going to inspire. Of course, I didn't know what it was I yearned to have happen. I didn't want to know. It had to happen of itself. It never did. In my room, I lay on my bed and fell asleep as it got dimmer and dimmer, and I'd wake up in darkness, not knowing where I was. Sundays in Louvain frightened me.

My intention was that Tom should feel, just a little, that I was doing him a favor by saying, Well, all right, I'll go with you to Brussels.

His voice gurgled. "Now we've got to find out about trains. How do we find out about trains? *Aller et retour,* don't forget. We should find out about return trains as well. I want this to be properly organized."

I said I'd ask my *bazin* if she had a train schedule. She did, in the top drawer of a chest with spiraling columns at the corners, inlaid with tortoiseshell, trimmed with swirling gilt. It was in her sitting room, where I knew she slept nights on the sofa, for I'd knocked on her door one morning and when she'd opened had seen, beyond the narrowly opened door, the rumpled sheets and blanket and pillow.

On the train, in a compartment to ourselves, Tom said, "Oh, by the way. You won't say anything to Karen about Pauline, will you? Not that there's any reason not to."

I shook my head.

He said, "I hope it doesn't rain."

"It looks like it."

"I hope not."

"It looks as if it will."

The train went past a garden bordered on either side by pollarded trees, and in the middle of the garden was a villa with a double staircase up to its main door and a hipped roof. All the windows of the villa were broken, and weeds were growing in the garden.

Tom asked me, "What stopped you from believing in God?"

"I don't want to talk about that," I answered.

"I'm sorry," he said. "But something did."

"Something did."

He tried to smile. "Whatever the experience was, I hope it was worth giving up your faith."

I leaned way back, my head pulling down the antimacassar.

Tom said, "I wish you could be happy. I wish you, especially you, could be enjoying, really enjoying, this year abroad — really, really enjoying a whole year's new experiences."

"I am enjoying them."

"You're not. And I wish I could make the difference."

"You?"

"You've got such an awareness of new experiences. But your awareness is despairing, and I'd like to think it could be joyful. We can talk to each other in this way. That's one good thing about our friendship. We don't have to say 'Hey' and 'Gee' to make ourselves out to be regular guys to each other. It means more to me than I can say that in talking to you I don't have to think about the way I'm talking in case one of the guys thinks I'm strange. You're brave not to care what anyone thinks about you. You make me want to be as brave, and not to care. You're brave, but I'm sorry for you. I'm sorry for you because no experience, however excitingly far it goes outside the commandments of God into another world, can be equal to the experience of God. Your awareness is despairing and it could easily be joyful."

The train shook. I looked over Tom's head, at the faded pictures of scenes in woods inserted into metal frames, and, above them, to the net of the luggage rack, sagging where someone had left an orange. Then I looked farther up to the blue light in the ceiling.

He asked me if I thought there was anything between Karen and Vincent, and I shrugged and looked away. The only time I spoke to him properly after what he had said to me was approaching the guard in the Brussels train station, when he said, "Now you've got to give him your ticket," and I said, "You have it," at which Tom stopped and searched through his pockets, patted his thighs and chest, wondering what he had done with my ticket. I was right — he had, when he'd bought the two, insisting he buy mine because this excursion was his treat, kept mine. I said, "You've probably got it with yours in your hand." He looked, he had, and he laughed and hit his head. I followed him out.

He entered into Brussels with the aplomb of someone who knew it well, knew all the cafés, restaurants, shops —

XIII

I WAS to his side, but just a step behind, as I followed Tom.

Brussels on a Sunday was not much different from Louvain, but bigger, so the emptiness of the streets and squares was bigger. It didn't rain, and the sun came out and beamed down into the empty squares and streets without casting shadows.

A trolley, empty except for its driver, was coming down the street, swaying from side to side as its metal wheels slithered in the tracks. We could have crossed before it got to us, but we waited for it to pass, and then we crossed.

"This way, this way," Tom said.

We went down business streets in which everything was shut. In the window of a clothes shop the dummies were naked, and stood still, holding out their arms in static, angular gestures toward one another. We turned corners.

"Now it should be just around the next corner to the right," Tom said.

We'd got to a residential street of large apartment buildings with their heavy doors shut. The doorknobs shone in the dull sunlight.

"It must have been to the left," Tom said.

We went to the left, and this too was a residential street. One car was parked in it, under a bare plane tree. A man came out of an apartment building and got into the car, and Tom and I watched him drive off.

"Oh Lord, Lord," Tom said. "I know, I know it's around here somewhere, the restaurant."

But he couldn't find it. I continued to follow him.

"If I could remember the name of it, I'd ask someone, if there was someone to ask," he said.

Then, walking from street to street, Tom with his head raised as if he were able to look over the tops of the buildings, out over the entire city, to see where the small restaurant was, we got lost. Around a corner was a big, blank, brick building, like a warehouse, and when Tom saw this he stopped as though in recognition of it, but no, it wasn't what he'd thought it was.

I didn't care if we didn't find the restaurant; I didn't want him to find it.

An idea occurred to him that would explain everything. "Of course," he said, "that's it: the restaurant is shut on Sunday, that's why we can't find it." He smiled.

"It doesn't matter," I said in a flat voice.

"But we'll find another place for lunch."

"I'm not hungry," I said in a flatter voice.

"No, no, we must eat. I invited you to lunch, and I'm going to make sure you have lunch." Again, raising his head to see over the city, he looked around. "We'll find a restaurant. We'll find one."

He walked off with the step of someone who now knew just where he was going, but I continued to follow a step behind.

We found ourselves in a working-class neighborhood of narrow gray cottages with net curtains over the windows, the front doors right on the pavement.

Tom said, "What we must do is ask someone who can tell us the way back to the station, and then I'll be oriented."

We walked along the street until we came to an empty lot, where, behind a chicken-wire fence, a little boy was digging. Tom held the wire fence and said to the little boy, *"Excusez-moi."* The boy looked up from his hole. *"La station,"* Tom asked, *"elle est où?"* The boy came to the wire fence and said something incomprehensible. Tom said to me, "He's speaking in Flemish." Again he asked the boy, enunciating clearly, *"Je voudrais savoir où est la station pour les trains."* The boy spoke in Flemish. Tom said to me, "He doesn't speak

French, but I think I understood him to say the station's back that way," and he pointed in the direction from which we'd come. We went back that way.

Tom said, "We could eat at the station buffet. They may have good food there. You know what gourmands the Belgians are. They may have very good food."

At every corner, he stopped to look in both directions before we crossed. He stopped at one corner to cross to the one directly ahead, and I suddenly crossed to the opposite corner while Tom was still looking both ways. I saw, when I reached the other corner, Tom look round for me, but I looked away. I walked along the opposite side of the street from Tom. Hurrying a little, he kept up with me on his side. Then I let him go ahead and fell behind him. Every time he'd look across the street at me, I'd look away. He was, I knew, aware of nothing else but me, not even of where he was going, as if his awareness of me precluded awareness of what we were doing lost in a city that was completely shut up. I was sure he was wishing I'd take over, I'd tell him to follow me, I'd find someone who'd give us directions. But I not only wouldn't do that, because it was all his responsibility, not mine, and I wanted him to know this; I couldn't do it, I was less capable than he of taking the lead.

Something occurred to me, and had occurred to me often enough in the past that I recognized it, as definite as a sudden, sharp headache: a sense of total removal from where I was, a sense of seeing across a long, long distance to an object, and a sense that I was also seeing through that object into a long, long distance behind it. And what was behind my sight, behind my eyes, went as far back in distance as what I saw before me. And what was behind me and what was before me in the far, far distances, beyond the world, was darkness. Tom was walking between these great dimensions of darkness, which curved out beyond him and the world as the concave sides of a sphere of universal dark. He was in the middle of it.

I didn't care that we were lost. I was fixed on Tom's big body in its bigger clothes, his tweed jacket and the scarf that he wore wound around his neck with the ends over his shoulders, as the students at Louvain wore theirs. I thought that in his big, awkward body, Tom had presumed on a right to live that he didn't have, Tom was totally vain. I hated the vanity of this presumption. I thought it was vain of him to be hungry (what right did he have to be hungry?), to be sleepy (what right did he have to be sleepy?), to have any bodily demands, even to want to pee and shit (he didn't have a right, and public toilets should be barred to him). And if Tom had any sexual desires, whatever they were, he should have no right to their fulfillment. There was justice in his not having been able to find the restaurant, as if he had no right to eat there. There was vanity in the shine of his black priest's shoes, in his chinos baggy at the bum, in the sagging pockets of his jacket, in the length of his hair, which he hadn't had cut since he'd arrived at the university. And he knew there was. Everything I saw about him he saw about himself, and I knew he saw it now, now at the moment I did, because I had the vision of there occurring all about him, as he stood at a street corner not sure which way to go and for an instant glancing at me, occurring like a bigger and more awkward version of himself standing at the middle of the dark universe, his awareness of himself as a fool. It wasn't because he was lost that he was a fool. He was always a fool. He was a fool in his very body. All he should want, all Tom should want, was to die.

Slowly he crossed the street toward me, slowly because he expected me to move to the opposite corner. His hands were clasped.

"I don't know what to do," he said.

I walked away. I didn't turn back to see if he was following me, but I knew he was. The direction I was going in had to be right, because office buildings appeared, and shops. And when I saw a man on a bicycle I raised my hand to halt him and asked him the way to the station, but I wasn't sure I followed his directions because I couldn't remember them. There were a few people strolling after their Sunday lunches, and I stopped them and asked again, and yet again. I knew

Tom was behind me, and I resented his seeing me ask directions again and again, as if I were no more capable of finding my way than he. I refused to look back, and when I was sure I knew my way I ran.

I wanted to leave him behind if I could. When I did turn, I didn't see him. The street behind me was empty.

I continued to run. I got to the station and realized Tom had my ticket, and I thought I should wait for him instead of spending money on another. But my impulse was to get away before he appeared, and I bought a second-class ticket and ran to the train, which was waiting.

In the compartment, the farthest forward there was, I slid the door shut and pulled the blind. I sat and bounced my head over and over against the headrest, which didn't have an antimacassar. At times I thought I must get up and go along the corridor to see if Tom was on the train. At other times I hoped he'd come find me, yet when I saw a face look in at the side window where I hadn't drawn the blind, a flash of hatred passed through me because I thought it was Tom come to look for me, but it was a middle-aged woman, who went away. The train started. I jumped up, slid open the door, opened the window in the corridor, and leaned out, but saw no one on the platform. I waited in the corridor for Tom to appear, and walked up and down the length of the carriage glancing into the compartments. Then I went back to my compartment and left the door open. Again I bounced my head against the headrest.

The sun was setting when the train reached the Louvain train station. Before it stopped, I was at the door, and when, with a jolt, it did stop, I banged open the door, jumped onto the platform, and ran along it to get out. But the guard asked for my ticket, and for a moment I thought I'd lost it, as I couldn't find it in my trouser pockets. It was in the breast pocket of my jacket. I handed it to the guard and rushed past the barrier.

XIV

I WOULD NEVER use about myself the words *despairing* and *joyful*, because these were states I believed I was not capable of, ever. And if I thought of joy as an affected state, I thought of despair as even more affected. I had never met anyone who had the right to use that word about himself, had only read about him, and this person, in whatever literature, seemed never to doubt that his despair was real, even if it was religious despair. I say "even if it was religious despair" because I thought that religion was the least reason for despairing, especially if you didn't believe in it. If you didn't believe, your despair had to be totally affected.

My greatest fear when I was young was that someone would think I was a phony. Tom was wrong when he said I didn't care what anyone thought about me, and I couldn't understand how he could have imagined that. It was not phony to be ironical, and I had tried to be ironical, but I came from a background that was so starkly unironical that being ironical was for me like taking on the manners of a foreigner, and that would make me phonier than ever.

When I got back to my room from Brussels, I lay on my bed in a state to which I refused to give any name, thinking that whatever name I gave it would give it an importance it didn't have. If it had to do with religion, it couldn't have a name, not for me, because religion meant nothing to me.

I slept, and woke in a dark room, and I knew that if a gun had been lying on a nightstand I would have picked it up, and without one thought or one feeling, I would have shot myself.

I turned on the light. There was nothing to eat for *souper* in my room. I usually kept bread and cheese and a bottle of mineral water. I didn't want to go out, even to the square across from the house, where there was a *frites* stand, which I could see from my window lit up by a row of white electric bulbs, and where three people were gathered.

I undressed and got into bed and turned off the light by the switch at the end of the cord dangling over the headboard.

Again something happened that had happened to me at times before, and I recognized it with the thought: Not this. I all at once twitched, so one arm rose up with a jerk and falling hit me in the face. Usually it happened to me when I went to bed hungry, and to make it stop all I had to do was get up and eat something. If I didn't eat, the spasms continued until dawn, when they stopped. It also happened to me when I was ill, especially with a fever.

My mental and, too, my emotional reaction to this was to be bored by it. I'd try to stop it by holding myself rigid, or, when the spasms became bad, by getting into positions that demanded more strain on my muscles than the spasms did. I would cross my arms and lie on them, and cross my legs at the knees and again at the ankles, and hold myself against the next spasm. My boredom became hatred of these fits, and I'd be determined to stop them. My arms and legs felt enormous and tingled because the flow of blood was blocked. Sometimes, if the spasm was bad, I would rise up on my knees, put my head on the mattress, and with my arms pull against my legs and with my legs pull against my arms, as much as I could, to make a rack of myself and draw into my exertion the energy that on its own was making my body do what I didn't want it to do; but that energy nevertheless took me over, for a spasm would unlock me from the most complicated rack and raise me up and fling me down. There was not a trace in this of anguish, much less of odd illumination. There was only the anxiety that it would go on all night and I wouldn't be able to sleep.

When it passed I always felt better, and I had come to consider these spasms as a cure, however tedious they were and however much I tried to stop them. As I didn't go to doctors, I never asked one about these nocturnal spasms, and in any case, I didn't think about them after I woke.

I thought: You've got to go out and eat something.

But I couldn't make myself get out of bed and dress and go out. I wasn't even hungry.

As if it were a presence in me that was building up its own energy to make me do what it wanted me to do, but to which I must appeal not to make me do that, I said out loud, "Go away, please go away, please let me sleep." The result of my appeal was a terrific spasm, one that, if I hadn't been under the blanket, would have thrown me off the bed. And this frightened me, not in itself, but because I didn't know how it would end.

I turned on the light, looked around the room, and thought it must be very late. I got up and looked out the window.

The *frites* stand was lit up, and a group of ten people or so were standing about it, eating their *frites* from paper cones.

A feeling came over me, like total intimidation, that I couldn't go out and buy any *frites,* for I might somehow make a fool of myself. I might make a mistake in French, might not understand the seller when he told me how much the *frites* cost, might drop my money. Also, he might wonder who I was and decide he didn't want to sell any *frites* to me, might decide I was a foreigner who had no rights in his country, not even to eat. And if I felt this intimidation about going out for *frites,* which I'd often bought, how much more did I feel about going out to a café, even the student café. I knew the seller of the *frites,* always said a few words to him when he handed them to me wrapped in a white paper cone through the little window of his stand, but it now seemed to me that knowing him made me more intimidated than if I hadn't, as the idea of going to the familiar student café, Alma's, where I might find myself having to ask the waitress I knew for hard-boiled eggs and mayonnaise, intimidated me more than the idea of going to a place where I'd never been, though I knew I couldn't do that either. Looking out the window, I didn't think, You've never felt this before, but You're feeling this again.

Once more I got into bed and shut off the light and sank under the covers, and once more, as if it had been waiting for me, that presence engorged my nervous system with more energy than it could stand and made me convulse.

I lit the light, I got up, I dressed. I walked about my room.

Soon it'd be too late to go out and get something to eat.

I turned my desk chair toward the window and looked out, beyond the net curtain, at the *frites* stand. There was only one person, and he walked away eating his *frites,* and as he walked away the electric bulbs went out, and only the dim inner light, which I could see through the small glass window that was now closed, remained.

Sweating, I put on my jacket and scarf and went out. It wasn't so late. I heard the creaking of the floors of the rooms of the other student lodgers as they walked about, and as I passed my *bazin*'s door I heard the faint sound of a radio. I shut the door to the street carefully.

I went to Tom's house. I stood before it and looked up. His windows were lit. I called up, "Tom." He didn't come. In a panic, I shouted, "Tom, Tom," and while I was shouting he came to a window, opened it, and leaned out. I heard him exclaim, "Oh." He drew his head in and disappeared and a moment later appeared and, leaning far out, threw down the four stories a white envelope with a key in it.

He met me at the top of the stairs to his room.

In his room, I said, "I'm not feeling well."

"What's wrong?"

"I don't know. Maybe I'd feel better if I had something to eat. I haven't eaten all day."

His head lowered, he hurried past me to his armoire. From it he took a wooden tray with a round Gouda cheese cut into by a knife, a roll of bread, a bottle of wine, a glass, and a plate. But he didn't seem to know what to do with the tray, for the table was being used as a desk. He went to it with the tray, couldn't put the tray on it for the books and papers, looked round for a place to put the tray, finally deposited it on his bed, cleared the table quickly by piling up all the books and papers on it at one end, pulled it out into the middle of the room, and placed the tray on it. Then he placed a chair before the table.

"It's all I have," he said.

I looked at it.

He spoke rapidly. "I had *souper* at Alma's with Karen, who's just back today, and Vincent. We were hoping you'd show up. I had a very, very good idea. I talked to Karen and Vincent about it. My idea is that we all go to Spain during our winter break. Vincent said that we could hire a car, that if we shared the cost it wouldn't be expensive. Don't you think it's a very, very good idea?"

Tom stopped speaking and drew out the chair for me to sit at the table.

I turned away. I went to his narrow bed, lengthwise against the wall, and lay on it, face down, and as soon as I lay flat a spasm shook me. I turned over.

"What's wrong?" Tom asked, coming to me, his voice high. "What is it?"

My arms twitched.

Tom kneeled by the bed to lean close to me.

I smiled at him. "It'll go."

"Are you sure?"

"Yes."

The next spasm made me rise up and put my arms around him and kiss him, kiss his forehead, cheeks, lips, chin, over and over. He didn't move. I let him go. I dropped back onto the bed.

He stood. "Can I do anything?" he asked.

"I don't think so."

"Is it anything that praying can stop?"

"No."

"But what else can I do?"

I closed my eyes.

I heard Tom take the chair from the table and move it toward me, but not very close, and sit on it. He asked, softly, "Do you want to spend the night here? I can sleep on the floor."

I opened my eyes and sat up. "No."

"As you haven't eaten anything all day, shouldn't you have something to eat?"

"I should." I got up.

He rose from the chair and again placed it at the table.

Quietly, I asked, "Would you mind if I took some cheese and that roll back to my room and ate there?"

"Of course not, of course not." With the knife he cut a wedge of cheese and said, "I'll wrap this and the roll in a piece of foolscap, how about that, so you can carry it." He handed me the badly wrapped package.

"Thanks," I said.

"You'll be all right? Maybe you should spend the night here. Or would you like me to come to your room with you? I could sleep in your armchair."

"I really will be all right," I said.

He picked up my scarf from the floor where it'd fallen and handed it to me and watched me, with my free hand, wrap it about my neck.

When I said goodnight and held out my hand to shake his, he, saying nothing, stepped back from me and placed his hands over his face as if to cover it.

XV

My greatest sins, I believed, had to do with my being a Franco-American, and were the sins of jealousy. Jealousy was one of our characteristics. Behind that expression *"Ça n' fait pas d' bon sens, là"* was the judgment on another who might be doing something original, individual, such as getting accepted into the Yankee university of Brown in Providence and studying history, and though the reason stated for its not making good sense to go to Brown and study history was that there was nothing to be done with history but teach it, the unstated reason was envy. Growing up in the parish, I often heard, in English with a Canuck accent, "Who does he think he is, that one there?" The envy was intense, but no one was aware of it, not even the *curé,* who never condemned it in a sermon.

I was so jealous of my freshman-year roommate in

college — he was better-looking than I, more intelligent, richer, more charming, so popular he was made president of the freshman class — I was jealous of his very sleep.

But my Franco jealousy went deeper, deep enough for me to have wished for the failure of everyone I'd ever been envious of, close friends especially — failure in their relationships, in their work, in their lives. For no other reason than that I'd been jealous of them, I'd wished people dead.

No one had a right to this will, and being thought special for having such a will and acting on it was a total presumption. The world that commended this will was a world of vanity. That anyone should realize his will and be honored for realizing it filled me with enough jealousy of his vanity that I would have liked to see his world end. And everyone was like that, everyone was presuming on the right to realize a will that, really, no one had a right to at all. And as I saw everyone's ego as nothing but presumptuous will, I condemned everyone for having an ego, for even being an individual with individual ideas of how the world should be governed and exploited, all to his individual benefit, as though this world, too, was his inalienable right. It wasn't, I thought, it wasn't.

At moments I found myself detached from my jealousy, and, as if in a sudden, clear space, thought: But I love everyone.

I had a vision of the world as I would have liked it to be, but as it wasn't. It was a world in which I did not have to be — have to be, as if I had no choice — jealous. That meant a world in which there was no one with the right, a right I myself didn't have, to realize his or her will, and no one, especially, who could impose his or her will on me, not even God. What everyone wanted, all together, would be what I wanted, in the most ideal form of communism ever thought of, a communism based not on principles but on an accord as natural, as innocent in its naturalness, as, as — And I would write in my diary about an island in the lake just off the point of land on which my family's summer cabin stood, a long, narrow island got to, with a few jumps across gaps, by a broken-down bridge made of old railway ties and rotting planks.

The earth of the island was held together by a dense tangle of wild vines and a few pine trees and scrub oaks, and it seemed to float on the placid lake. My possession of the island meant I had to take care of it, and I removed from it and around it all the slimy green bottles, corroded tin cans, worn tires, coils of rusted wire, and automobile parts that had for years been dumped on it or thrown from passing boats. I wanted the island to be completely natural, wanted to return it to the state I imagined it had been in before any humans had stepped onto it, as though any sign of a human being there could only make the island unnatural. The

Indians wouldn't have left a trace of themselves, but would have been as if invisible among the trees. I collected a great amount of refuse in bags as I walked about, pushing aside the vines with a stick, and hauled the refuse back to what I called the mainland, to be taken away by the garbage man to I had no idea what human and horrible place. In old sneakers, I walked in the water around the island — which did, I discovered, float, for its edge of roots and plants extended out over the water — and I reached under its edge, among blue gill, to pull out more refuse, which I collected in a potato sack tied to an inflated inner tube I pulled along behind me with a length of rope. Sometimes strangers would go to the island at night while I was asleep and light a fire, and the next day I'd find their trash around the ashes of a small tree they'd cut down, and I would clean up the trash and scatter the ashes. Sometimes there was a half-burned condom in the ashes.

I wanted that island to be pure, to be, in its naturalness, innocent, and I wanted this to be the world.

Was there any way I could confess my sins and receive absolution and become pure? To admit a sin was not to be forgiven it. I admitted my sins, the greatest of which — derived, I was sure, from my destructive envy — was despair. But when I recalled preparing for confession in the pew of the church; when I thought of the shame of examining my conscience for all the sins committed, a shame that made me sweat; when I thought of the strange jerk in me when it was my turn to go to the confessional and the walk along the length of the pew, sometimes stepping on the kneeler; and when I thought of the dimness of the confessional and the ear behind the grille; and when I thought of the forgiveness, which occurred the moment the priest raised his hand to bless me, and the walk back to the pew, knowing I was now pure, now innocent, like that island I so wanted to keep pure and innocent; when I thought of that state of grace, I —

No, it wasn't possible.

XVI

EVERY NIGHT for almost a week the spasms kept me from sleeping until dawn, and then I would sleep until noon. In the afternoon I'd eat part of a meat pie in my room and in the evening I'd eat the other part.

There was a knock on my door one early afternoon, and I opened and saw my *bazin* and, behind her, Karen.

Leaving us, my *bazin* began to close the door. I told her to leave it open. She left it ajar.

In my room, Karen looked at a framed watercolor by the door of a sunset through pine trees. I felt she had come to talk to me, and I waited for her to turn away from the picture to me. She did and said, "Let's get out of your room and walk around the town."

For a while we walked in silence, from time to time pointing out a detail of architecture on a chimney or gable or architrave to each other.

When she said, "I want to talk to you about something," I felt a little shiver go through me.

I asked, "About what?"

"Tom is worried about you."

As if I had half known it was Tom she wanted to talk to me about and it was half knowing this that had caused the shiver, I felt, now, a great thrill.

She said, "My feeling is that Tom indulges you. He wouldn't worry about you if he didn't indulge you."

"Indulges me?"

"If you're depressed, you should do something about it."

"Who told you I'm depressed? Tom?"

"No. Tom didn't even say he was worried about you. I can tell just by the way he says he hasn't seen you in a while that he's worried. And I can tell just by seeing you that you're depressed."

I was interested. "What do you see?"

"You'd like to know, wouldn't you? You like knowing people think you're depressed. You like knowing Tom is worried about you. You're interested in yourself."

"I don't know if I am," I said, and looked away.

"I think you are," she said. She stopped. "Look at me."

I looked her in the eyes. She said to me, "Why am I suspicious of you?" I continued to stare at her, but it seemed to me she sank far back from me and her voice came from a distance. "Why don't I believe you?"

"Believe me?"

"There is something phony about you, you know. I'm not sure your depression is as dark as you like to think it is. You want to think it's dark, deeply, deeply dark, for some reason. I don't know what your reason could be. Maybe you think that's the only way you have of impressing people, of convincing them you're not phony. Maybe. I don't know you well enough. Whatever your reason, it doesn't convince."

As she spoke, Karen appeared to go farther away from me and become smaller and smaller, her voice also, and yet it seemed to me she had the right to say anything she wanted to me, and I had to accept it. I had been accused in the same way in the past, in America, and I had always had to accept the accusations.

Karen asked me, "What real reason do you have for being depressed?"

I wanted to say, Not depressed, in despair, and the despair had possessed me, in the way I believed God, to prove His existence, must possess. I could never use the word *despair* with Karen; she would laugh, would say, in a mocking voice, "Despair?" I couldn't tell her: "I despair because God will not make this world His."

I said to Karen, "I don't have any reason."

She sank so far back she seemed to disappear.

She said, "Tom is worried about you because he doesn't want you to stay here in Louvain on your own during the winter break. He's thinking of staying, too, if you stay. He'd like you to come to Spain with us. You'd make him feel happy if you said you'd come."

"Feel happy?" I asked.

"Yes."

"Of course I want Tom to feel happy."

Karen said, "I know you and Tom and Vincent don't have much money. I do. I'll pay for the rental of the car, and I won't mind staying in cheap hotels."

I said, "You're doing this for Tom, aren't you?"

"Yes," she said frankly. "I don't know if I'd do it for you. I'm doing it because unless you come, Tom won't feel right, and I want him to feel right and well. He's been upset lately. He keeps saying, 'Uh, uh, uh,' as if he's become stupid. I know it has to do with you. He only said you didn't want to see him. I can't be forward with Tom, but I can with you. What did you do that upset him? It couldn't have been Tom who did anything."

I shrugged.

Impatient, she said, "It doesn't matter. What matters is that he's frightened for you. Maybe he's even frightened of you. I'm not. I think I understand you well enough. You're the kind of person who tries to get people to believe in him by saying he wants to die, and I know you're as far away as the sun from wanting to die. But Tom would believe it. Don't do that to Tom. I told him to send you a letter to ask you if you'd come to Spain. Answer it that you will."

This note from Tom was put through the mail slot:

I hope you can come next week to Spain. Karen and Vincent do, too.

Your friend,
Tom

It wasn't Tom wanting me to go to Spain, but Spain itself, where I couldn't at all imagine being with Tom or even with Karen and Vincent, that made me think: Yes, I want to go.

I would get out of Louvain and I would get out of the state I was in by going to Spain. Whenever I thought of visiting a place, I never thought about the particulars of it: what hotel I would stay in, or that meals and entrances to museums and theaters cost money. It seemed to me that in a far place you didn't stay in any particular hotel, didn't eat in any particular restaurant, and nothing cost money.

I thought: Tom's trying to help me, and I appreciate that, but really, he doesn't, and can't, understand.

I went to Tom's, but he was out. His *bazin,* shaking almost as much as I did when I threw a fit, asked me if I wanted to leave a message, and I said only that I'd stopped by. I was relieved he was out, and I realized I didn't want to see him.

And I kept wondering what, after the night I'd gone to his room, he thought about me. I kept wondering, and at moments I'd tell myself, You don't care what he thinks, you don't care what anyone thinks about you. Wherever he was, Tom must have been thinking,

What's wrong with him? There was nothing wrong with me, I wanted to tell him. I didn't want him to think anything at all about me. All my thinking, no matter what it was about, was such that I'd break into it again and again, more and more, to break it up entirely, with: You don't care about that, you don't care what anyone thinks, not anyone, and especially not Tom.

But I had to go to Spain with Tom. I couldn't have gone to Spain without him, I needed him to get me there.

Hoping not to meet him, I walked about the university area of the town looking for him.

I passed a round lecture amphitheater and saw, outside the closed doors, a large group of students, the ones at the doorway banging on it with their fists, and all of them shouting. They were trying to get in. Why they were, and why they were shut out, I had no idea, until I realized that a Catholic philosopher was to lecture there at this time. The amphitheater was packed, the doors had been closed. I didn't see Tom among the ones demonstrating to get in. He would have arrived early and got a seat.

I realized, too, that I did not at all understand why anyone should be passionate — as the students trying to get in were — about listening to the ideas of a man, passionate enough to believe those ideas would make a difference to him. Tom was like that. I wasn't.

Though we were both from working-class Catholic backgrounds, there were essential differences between Tom and me, and one was that Tom had a sense of an intellectual whole, a system, he could believe in, and I didn't. My background was more primitive than Tom's: after centuries in the Canadian forests, my family had not only lost all sense of an intellectual whole, of any system, they were hardly capable of conceiving ideas.

Tom was an intellectual. I wasn't. If I had been Tom, I would, even without believing in God, have loved Louvain. But Tom believed in God.

I went into the park and passed the tower and went out the park at the other end. In a little square with a stone monument in the middle was Vincent. He waved at me as I approached him. He said that he was waiting for Karen to have lunch and that I should join them.

"You're feeling all right now?" he asked.

"I am."

"Will you be able to come to Spain with us?"

I hesitated. I said, "Tom said he wouldn't go without me."

Vincent, his face pale and his eyes black, stepped away from me when he saw Karen coming across the square.

"I'm glad you're better," she said to me. She smiled in a slightly crooked way because of the scar on her lower lip.

I joined them for lunch in a restaurant that was expensive for the Belgian students, but wasn't for us American students.

Karen said all she would eat was a *bifteck américain,* a pat of raw ground beef with a raw egg on the top of it. She was trying to lose weight before going to Spain. She wouldn't even have wine.

"I always feel I've got to be looking my best when I travel," she said.

She took a drink from Vincent's glass of wine.

"So, have you told Tom you'll come to Spain?" she asked me.

"I guess I like to play games with Tom," I said. "I've kept him guessing."

"I can understand wanting to do that," Karen said, and laughed and took a sip of wine from Vincent's glass.

"Did he tell you about our excursion to Brussels?" I asked. They said no, and for a moment I wondered if I should tell them. "I felt I was in that city for eternity, following big, plump Tom pointing down streets and saying, *This way,* and getting more and more lost. You should have seen him trying to communicate through a chicken-wire fence with a little boy in an empty lot who could only speak Flemish —"

Karen laughed, and Vincent, who never laughed, smiled. Even when Vincent smiled his eyes were stark.

He said, "I hope eternity for me is more interesting

than following Tom, lost, around the streets of Brussels. Anyway, I don't have any doubts I'll be going to hell, and I know Tom won't be there."

"How do you know Tom doesn't have a secret life?" Karen asked. "Like you?"

Vincent pressed his lips together to smile in a wicked way, and Karen returned the smile.

Vincent had bought a natty European suit, which he wore all the time. I should have been, for his good looks, his sartorial smartness, his secretiveness, jealous of him, but I wasn't.

XVII

VINCENT SAID he and Karen would be outside my door at five o'clock on Thursday, in three days, with the rented car. He'd tell Tom to come to my room to wait there, as I was on the way out of town. I realized I hadn't actually said I'd go to Spain.

At the lecture in philosophy the day before we left, which I went to hoping to see him, I didn't see Tom, and at the student café or the restaurant we usually went to for lunch I didn't see him, though I was always prepared for our encounter. I would act as if nothing had happened between us, not even that he'd sent me a note, and I'd let him think I'd never been in doubt about going to Spain.

The evening before we left, I had *souper* with Vincent and Karen. Vincent said he'd told Tom to join us, but Tom didn't come. Going home, I went out of my way to pass the house he lived in and stood and looked up at his lighted windows and was about to call up to him, but, just as you might look down and tell yourself to jump from a not very great height and decide you can't, I didn't call him. The night was misty.

If I ate a lot of bread at my *souper* and didn't drink alcohol, not even beer, my spasms weren't violent, and though I'd wake up from time to time with a twitch I'd sleep more than not. The spasms occurred then in my dreams, which were violent, and these, too, sometimes woke me. During the day, I didn't think about the nights.

Packing my suitcase, I found, thrown at the back of my armoire, a sport shirt I'd worn in Spain. It hadn't been washed and smelled of sweat and suntan lotion and sea salt. I put it over my face and breathed through it.

I felt a spasm when, in the afternoon, I heard the doorbell ring and I knew it was Tom. Again I prepared myself as I went downstairs. My *bazin* had opened the door and was talking to him in the entry, where he stood with his suitcase by his side and his overcoat collar turned up and his scarf wound round and round the outside of the collar. His face was red. He said to me, *"Je viens de dire à Madame qu'elle doit venir en Espagne avec nous."* Madame seemed to think this was a sincere invitation, for she protested that she couldn't, she had the other students to cater to, and besides, she had her cat, who would take care of her cat? *"Ah non, monsieur, non, j' puis pas."* But she was nevertheless excited to have been proposed such an impossible invitation. She'd never even been to Paris. *"Non, non,"* she continued, *"vraiment, non."* She said she'd bring Monsieur Tom and me some hot chocolate before our long trip. I held out my hand to Tom to indicate he should go ahead of me up the stairs.

When he lifted his suitcase, my *bazin* told him to leave it in the entry, but he thought that it might be in the way there, and she reassured him it wouldn't, though perhaps he was worried that it wouldn't be secure there, and he said no, no, it wasn't that, he was sure it would be secure, only it might be in the way, for supposing someone came in with, *disons,* a table and found it in the way, and she said no one was going to come in with a table — Why, I asked myself, does he always have to complicate everything? In the end, he left it, shoved flat against the wall, and by then I had gone up the stairs ahead of him to my room, feeling irritation at him for his always messing everything up.

Once in my room, I felt my embarrassment toward him return, and I spoke and acted in broad ways, like telling him to take off his overcoat, throw it on the bed, sit in the armchair, while I, I said, finished a letter to my parents, if he didn't mind. I hadn't thought of writing, but did while Tom sat quietly.

As I wrote, or attempted to, I from time to time

glanced at Tom, his head down as if meditating. Once, I glanced up and our eyes met. He kept looking at me. I felt as different from him as if I still lived within my family and had no life outside it. I saw Tom as a stranger standing outside and looking through the branches of trees into woods where I was a native among natives.

In his presence, I couldn't write to my parents. Tom always did this, had done it even before that evening in his room: made me think I didn't know how to do anything and feel everything I tried to do I did for the wrong reasons. Tom crossed and uncrossed his legs. I kept up the pretense of the letter until my *bazin* came in with the hot chocolate.

Tom said, at least ten times (I would have said to Karen and Vincent, at least a million times), how good the hot chocolate was, and he ran his baby-pink tongue over his upper lip, but he held out his hand and said, "No, no," when I told him to take more. "There's almost half a pot left," I said, "and my *bazin* won't know what to do with it." "All right, then," he said, "just half a cup." I poured it out.

Watching it stream into the cup he held up, he said, "I've got an aunt who says, every time you ask her for only half a cup of tea, 'Top half or bottom half?' " He looked up at me and smiled, looked into my eyes, and I felt all my embarrassment leave me, and I smiled back.

"She sounds like a woman I'd like," I said.

"Oh, everyone likes her."

But the sudden openness between us lasted only a moment, for we went silent, he in the armchair, I on my desk chair, and we concentrated on our hands holding the cups.

By drinking the hot chocolate as though it were the most delicious drink in the world, Tom was determined not to let the silence between us become fixed. He wanted us to be talkative, open, and spontaneous with each other, and he was trying to think of something to say other than, once again, how delicious the hot chocolate was, to unfix our closed, studied silence. He was suffering because he couldn't think of anything. The embarrassment seemed to be all his, not at all mine, and he had the responsibility to excuse himself from having done something embarrassing, excuse himself without referring to what he had done, by introducing a subject, something that had nothing to do with us personally, that'd be a relief to me and in that way to him, something I'd find funny, because the subject shouldn't be serious, not now. Tom didn't know that he in himself was funny to me, but only when I was talking about him to others, for though I felt when I was with him that I should be amused by him, I felt that what made him amusing annoyed me.

"Oh, I know," he said. He laughed. "You remember that Pauline said she went every Sunday to talk to a

Flemish woman and pray with her? Well, that old, pious woman taught her an expression in Flemish that shocked, really shocked some priests when Pauline, not knowing what it meant, repeated it to them, it was so blasphemous." His laughter twisted in his throat, and he coughed.

I tried to smile.

Again we went silent, and again I saw that look of ridiculous suffering on his face as he tried to think of something else to tell me.

I got up and went to the window to glance out. "They should be here," I said.

I turned back and saw Tom's face.

He said, "I want to help you. I do."

I stepped toward him, stopped, and said, "I know you do."

A car horn sounded. I turned to the window and saw, in the street below, the little car, its two doors open, with Karen standing on the far side and waving at me and Vincent looking up from the driver's seat.

I heard Tom say in a bright voice, "We'd better go."

Standing, he was smiling at me, a wide smile.

"We'd better get on our way," he said. As though I, motionless, were reluctant to leave, he said, "Come on, let's get going."

The idea occurred to me that his excitement came from his realizing that after all he was stronger than I, that I was weak, and if I was reluctant to go with him it was because I didn't want him to know I'd given in to him. I had given in to him, but I hoped, by fussing with my coat and scarf and valise, that he would think I was occupied with what was more important. I cleared my throat often.

I held my bedroom door open for him.

"We're going, we're going," he said, and his voice broke like that of an adolescent boy trying to sing.

My *bazin* was at the door of her quarters as Tom and I descended. She asked me if she should put the hot chocolate on my bill, but didn't wait for a response, as she was more excited than we were about our going to Spain. She said to Tom, *"N'oubliez pas votre valise,"* and I thought, as a matter of fact he was capable of forgetting a valise. He thanked her and took it. I shifted mine from one hand to the other. She opened the door to the street for us.

Vincent got out of the car to lift the hood, so we could put the valises in. Mine was bigger than anyone else's, and as Vincent tried to get it in with the others, complaining to Karen, Tom and I watched; he managed to wedge it in, then he shut the hood, which was so thin it wobbled when he slammed it. The two doors of the car were open. Vincent got into the driver's seat, and Karen stood by the door of the front passenger seat.

She asked Tom, "Where do you want to sit?"

"It doesn't matter," he said.

"Tell me."

"You tell me where you want to sit, and I'll tell you where I'll sit."

"You tell me."

I asked, "Does it make any difference?"

"It makes all the difference," Karen said. "I want him to make up his mind."

Vincent said, "Will you all get in?"

Tom said, "No one thinks I have a mind of my own. It's quite true, I don't. I don't know where I want to sit."

"God damn it," Vincent said, "sit in the back seat."

Tom said to me, "You get in first."

"No, no," I said, "you get in."

Again Vincent shouted at Tom, not at me, "Get in and be quiet."

Karen held the front seat up for Tom to get in and slide to the other side of the car, behind Vincent. "I'll be quiet," he said, adjusting his body to the small space. "You'll see."

I folded myself up and got in.

Rain began to fall as soon as we left Louvain.

Turning her head round, Karen said to Tom, "Tell me about the lecture by Étienne Gilson."

Vincent groaned. He said, "You didn't have to do that, did you?"

Tom pointed to Vincent, then placed his fingers over a half-smile.

"Tell us," Karen said, "tell us."

Tom did, till it was dark and the windshield wipers swept in arcs across the glass to reveal nothing but more rain falling on it and running down in rivulets before the wipers swept across again. From time to time there appeared through the rain the yellow lights of an oncoming car.

I don't recall how long it took us to get to the French border, but more than three hours. The little car's small wheels were rotating at what was for it a very great speed. Gusts of rain-laden wind made it sway. In France, we thought we'd soon be in Paris.

We were on a three-lane highway, the middle lane meant to be used only for passing. Vincent accelerated and pulled out to pass a car, but coming toward us, fast, was a car in the middle lane passing a car farther behind, and as it pulled into its lane Vincent pulled quickly into ours and then braked, and our little car, sliding as if on wet leaves, spun around completely and faced back in the direction of Louvain. We sat for a while in silence, then Vincent turned and we continued on to Paris.

We became excited then, and joked. Our jokes were silly. I opened a bottle of wine that Karen had brought with the corkscrew she'd also brought, and handed her the bottle. She swigged from it, handed it back and I swigged, and I handed it to Tom. Vincent shook his head no when Tom, after swigging, held the bottle over his shoulder. Karen took it. Vincent was the only one of us who wasn't joking, but, leaning over the steering wheel, he seemed to be driving the car on his concentration alone. The more he concentrated, the faster he could make the car go. From my angle in the back seat, I saw the sharp, pale outline of the side of his face and the corner of his right eye, almost closed as he appeared not so much to stare out as to think intently. Tom asked for the bottle of wine, which Karen had.

The rain streamed in sheets down the windshield, and the yellow lights of oncoming cars appeared to waver through the sheets, then become closer for a second when the wipers cleared the glass, then again blur in the rain. Drafts blew in as if there were no bottom to the car and our feet were raised just a little above the wet, black, asphalted highway we sped over.

Vincent pulled out to pass a car, and as he was passing it I saw, coming toward us in the same lane, a truck with large yellow headlights and two smaller lights and the high, wide windshield of the cab. The yellow lights appeared to be vibrating. We all went silent and leaned forward to look, Tom grasping the back of Vincent's seat with one hand.

A very, very long time passed, long enough to get to Paris, to get anywhere, and as it passed we were calmly, clearly aware that it would end when we hit the truck, and we would die.

I stared at those vibrating yellow lights.

On impact, my head was jerked forward and my face, at the level of my eyes, hit something hard. I kept my eyes closed.

After the impact there was again a long, long time that passed, the silent calm.

You don't feel any pain yet, I thought, but if you've lost an arm or a leg there are good ones made today, and if you've lost an eye there are good, lifelike glass eyes —

Slumped forward, I opened my eyes and half saw dark bodies, also slumped. Tom's hand was holding onto the back of Vincent's seat.

I heard voices outside that sounded very distant, then suddenly close when the car doors were opened. A man said, *"Ne bougez pas, ne bougez pas,"* and I felt arms about me and a man's voice in my ear saying, *"Ne bougez pas."* I was carried by two men and laid on a blanket or overcoat on the ground, and as I lay I felt rain on my face.

If I was alive, so were the others. And yet they seemed far, far from me, so far they couldn't have been in the same accident as I. If there had been others in this accident, they weren't Karen and Vincent and Tom, not quite, but others, people I didn't really know, whom I might never see again.

I was placed on the floor of what looked, when I opened my eyes for a moment, like an internally illuminated bus. It was empty except for two passengers sitting in seats distant from each other. The hand straps shook as the bus drove off. One of the passengers had long, tangled blond hair, and the other, toward the front, was hunched forward, and had short black hair. Another passenger was placed flat along the back seat of the bus. I closed my eyes.

I opened them again in the emergency room of a small hospital. I was the first to be taken in and laid on an examination table. Vincent walked in and leaned against a wall, his hands to his stomach. Groaning, he lowered his head, his black hair sticking out. I saw Karen come in and stand behind an examination table, her hair undone, blood dripping from her lower lip. She looked at me and smiled.

I laughed.

There were people in white, including a nun in a white habit with a huge white wimple, but they moved about as if they had nothing to do with us.

Before Tom could be taken in, I was taken out.

My bed was narrow and hard, and I was not allowed a pillow. I rolled my bandaged head back and forth. The dim overhead lights were on in the small ward, where men in their beds stared at the black windows.

Beyond the open double doors of the ward was a long passage, and rolling my head that way, I saw a stretcher being wheeled into a room off the passage.

All night I heard Vincent's screams. Even at a distance, he kept the ward I was in awake. I heard, *"Ah, mais c'est assez, ça, c'est assez,"* from different men, who turned in their narrow metal-frame beds.

Woken by a flashlight held close to my face, I felt my body jump, and I called out, "Who is it?" It was a nurse in a white cap.

I had to lie flat for some days, and I assumed the others, too, were in their beds. Every night Vincent, in his part of the hospital, screamed. He shouted, too, over and over, *"Mon estomac, mon estomac,"* pronouncing the *c*. From time to time during the night a nurse shone a flashlight in my face.

One morning Karen came to my bed and told me Tom was dead.

XVIII

KAREN'S FATHER came to the hospital and drove her away to Paris to stay in a grand hotel. From Paris she took a local train every day to Gonesse, where the provincial hospital was, to visit Vincent and me.

Vincent was badly injured. He slept during the days and shouted, as ever, during the nights.

The nurse with the flashlight asked me if I'd stay with him at night to try to calm him. I said yes, and she wheeled me into his lit room. He appeared to be suspended by wires and pulleys over a high iron bed. An arm in plaster was raised above his head. His body was covered with a loose sheet. The nurse left me in the wheelchair by him.

He looked at me, then away, and he began to jerk. As he jerked, the sheet slipped off, and I saw he had a draining tube in his stomach and another in his penis.

His body was sweating. He looked at me again, and his face contorted, but he didn't shout. I touched his naked thigh.

When it was time for me to leave the hospital, Karen came for me in a rented car and drove me back to Louvain, where she, too, returned to live.

Madame my *bazin* prepared a bath for me, and when it was ready knocked on my door. I went down, through cold stairwells and passageways, to the back garden, and from there down into the cellar. Blankets had been hung on lines to enclose a dim space with a tin tub of hot water, buckets of cold water, and a large tin drum, at the bottom of which red flames showed and made a muted roar in the underground silence. I put my clothes, with a clean change of underwear and socks, on the seat of a chair. When I poured cold water from a bucket into the hot water of the tub, steam rose. I sat in the tub, and the displaced water came up to my waist. I closed my eyes for a moment, then began to wash. I washed an arm over and over.

A note came from Tom's *bazin* through mine to please go see her. I didn't go, as I thought I wouldn't be able to make my way.

The first time I went out was with Karen to the university chapel for a Mass said for Tom. On a table in the foyer of the chapel memorial cards were spread out; they were edged in black and had Tom's photograph on them. I glanced at them, at the many reproductions of Tom's face, fat, with wavy black hair, smiling a little. This was his passport photograph. I didn't take a card.

I followed Karen inside the chapel, but not to the front where she went; I stayed at the back, chose a chair away from others, turned it around, and knelt on it.

The church had paintings in wide gilt frames, but because of the penetrating cold coming from the stone walls, it seemed as if these were transparent and the gray, stark blocks of the walls showed through from behind them. The cold stone paving of the floor appeared to show up through transparent caned chairs, as the arches showed down through the crystal chandeliers.

When I saw the priest, in a black-and-silver embroidered chasuble, enter and go to the altar, I put my hands over my face.

While I knelt, my hands over my face, hearing the Mass for the Dead, I felt I was in darkness.

I heard, *". . . que votre lumière les éclaire à jamais,"* and I felt a movement, as of suddenly falling through the darkness, and as I fell I realized that I was dead. Not Tom but I had died, and Tom, alive, was standing on the earth, smiling and watching me fall.

I began to weep. My hands were covered in my tears, which I pressed against my face.

I heard, *". . . faites-les passer, Seigneur, de la mort à la vie,"* and falling farther and farther away, I sobbed for

Tom, who remained in the world, and who believed in the world as he believed in God. Tom's God was bright, and gave light to the world. My God was different: was the darkness around the world.

It was as though Tom, whom I had always imagined able to take care of himself, had made a choice to stay on the earth, and I, unable to help myself, had let go. And as I fell, backward so I saw the world become rounder and rounder and brighter and brighter as I fell, I pitied Tom for staying, for being the one with the choice.

I pitied him for his love for the world. I pitied him for his bright love for God.

I kept my head lowered until the Mass was over, and when I raised it I saw the church was empty.

My legs shook as I walked out to the stone-paved area before the church.

Karen and Pauline were standing together. I hadn't been aware they knew each other. As I went toward them they stopped talking. Karen's eyes were filled with tears. Pauline said, a corner of her mouth raised:

"It had to be Tom."

Karen reached out a hand to take me by the arm, and leaning closer, she pressed her face against my shoulder.

When she drew back, I asked, "What do you want to do?"

"You tell me, please."

"We'll go for a walk."

I asked Pauline if she wanted to come too. She checked her watch and said she had an hour, so she'd come.

I walked between the two women, Karen's arm in mine.

The sky looked as if it were over an ocean.

Pauline said, "Tom used to confide in me."

From deep in her throat, Karen said, "Oh?"

"He was worried about what he was going to do in his life. I kept telling him his life was in the Church, and I almost convinced him he had it in him to be a missionary."

Karen again said quietly, "Oh?" as a way of letting Pauline know she was at least being attentive, a little.

"One of those missionaries you see walking around Louvain in white robes and with strings of big black beads around their necks."

Pauline continued to talk about Tom and these missionaries, and I felt in Karen, close to me, a mutual accord to let Pauline take over Tom, if that was what she was claiming.

After half an hour, Pauline, checking her watch again, said she had to go.

Karen and I bought food and went to my room to eat it. She was with me, both of us by the coal stove, when Tom's *bazin* arrived to see me. She was agitated, and this made her shake more than ever; her hands, which were red and appeared to be wet, moved all about her body as though she wanted to touch herself but couldn't. She said that Monsieur Tom had taken his room for a full scholastic year, but hadn't paid for the year. He was a good boy, Monsieur Tom, but what would she do if she didn't have her rent? It was too late to find someone to take it now.

Karen said she'd pay the rent. Then she said she'd take the room.

Was that permitted? the *bazin* asked.

Karen said yes, she'd make sure it was.

After she moved in, on a Sunday afternoon, Karen and I wandered about Louvain, about the empty streets, stopping to look in shop windows.

She said, "I've got a headache. I've had it since I moved into that room."

"You think it has to do with the room?" I asked.

"Maybe."

We walked down a narrow cobbled street, through a stone-arched passageway, into a wider cobbled street, past an old step-gabled house between the buttresses of an old church. Up the street, an old man was riding a bicycle away from us.

"If we went to your room," Karen asked me, "would your *bazin* prepare us some hot chocolate?"

"We'll find a pastry shop open and we'll buy some pastries to have with our hot chocolate."

"All the pastry shops are shut," she said.

"We'll find one open," I insisted.

Karen sat in the armchair by the coal stove while I took from the tray that my *bazin* held the spoons and cups and pot of hot chocolate and put them on my desk. Down the white porcelain side of the pot ran a brown drip.

My *bazin* stood back with the tray and asked if there was anything else I wanted.

No, I said, and thanked her.

She hesitated. Did I want her to add this to the bill?

Yes, please.

Very well, she agreed, but she remained, gray, in a gray dress, holding the tray as if it were still charged with things. She seemed to want to say something more. Leaving, she began, as she did each time Karen was in my room, to close the door. Karen told her it wasn't necessary to close it. As always, she left it half open.

I gave Karen a cup of chocolate and a flaky pastry on a little white plate. From one end of the pastry oozed custard. With mine, I sat on the chair at my desk. Karen put her plate with the uneaten pastry and the cup of chocolate on the floor, then leaned back in the armchair.

"I don't feel well," she said.

"What is it?"

"I feel weak."

"Lie on my bed."

She did, she lay on the brown-yellow spread, and pulled the pillows and bolster out from under it to lean her head and shoulders on them.

Outside, boys shouted at one another in the square.

"I think I have a fever," Karen said.

I went to the bed and put my hand on her forehead.

"Do I?"

"No."

"You know, I feel that I have something really wrong with me."

"If you feel so bad, I'm going to get my *bazin* to call a doctor.

Lifting her head from the pillow, she said, "No, no, I'm not that bad. I'll close my eyes for ten minutes, and then I'll feel better."

"Do you want me to leave you alone?"

"I don't want you to, no, but maybe you want to be alone."

"No. I'll sit at my desk and read."

I did, my back to her. The room got dark, and I switched on my desk lamp. When I heard her call my name, I closed the book and turned to her.

"How are you?" I asked.

"Better, I think," she said.

"It's almost time to eat," I said. "We can go to a café."

"I don't want to eat. I don't want to do anything. I think I'll go back to my room."

"But that room makes you feel bad."

"I'll get over it," she said.

She remained lying on the bed.

I said, "Don't go. Let's do something together."

"Oh, I don't know if I feel much like doing anything."

"I think you should. I think we should."

"I'm going back to my room," she said, and she got up, put on her coat, and left.

She didn't come to me during the week. The next Sunday, in the morning, I visited her. She lay on that narrow, sagging bed pushed lengthwise against the wall. I told her she should get out, we should both get out, and I proposed we go to Brussels for the day. She said she didn't want to, but I insisted, and she, pulling her hair away from her face, finally said all right, she'd come.

In the train compartment, sitting by my side and studying a street map of Brussels, Karen said to me, "I'm glad you made me come."

"You see," I said.

"I'm not going to let that accident make me sick."

"You can't," I said. "You can't."

In Brussels, we went down a side street, which became an alley, to the end, where there was a small restaurant with a menu, mimeograph-purple, posted in the window.

"They have eel as a specialty," I said. "I've never had eel."

We were served bowls of stewed eels in green-gray broth.

After I lifted the spoon to my lips and sipped the broth, "Oh," I said, "it's delicious."

She must have realized that, false in my enthusiasm as I was, I was being false for her. She tasted the eel stew. "It is, yes," she said, falsely. "Oh, yes, it is."

When we left, Karen leaned against a wall.

"What's the matter?" I asked.

"Nothing," she said. "I must have drunk too much wine."

"Let's go down this street," I said.

At the opening where the street ended was a crowd, and over the heads of the crowd passed large upright white ostrich feathers. I pressed my way through the people lining the curb, and made a space for Karen to stand before me. Men were dancing down the street. They wore red costumes covered with white beads, and great, white, bobbing and twisting ostrich feather headdresses, and they juggled oranges. Oranges rolled in the street. Children picked them up and threw them, anywhere. The windows of the shopfronts had their grilles down, and the shutters of the houses were closed. Whenever an orange was thrown up, everyone followed it up until it began to fall, and then all lowered their heads and hunched their shoulders, and some women shouted. Here and there in the crowd raised hands caught falling oranges. About us, the air was cold and gray.

An orange rolled toward me, and I went out into the street to pick it up. Karen flinched when I threw the orange toward her, but she caught it.

"Throw it back," I said.

Trying to smile, she held the orange out to me.

"Throw it."

Karen lowered her arm.

I went to her. "It's no good," I said.

"No," she said.

XIX

VINCENT WAS in the hospital for over a month. I visited him only once. I couldn't afford to rent a car, so visiting him required going to Paris by train, then taking another, local train. He was in a bed in the men's ward. He said he hadn't seen Karen. Had I? I hadn't, I said, not for a while.

I went to lectures when they resumed, and to them and from them walked through the narrow park where there was always mist in the bushes. Two paths went through the park, one on a low level, one on a high, each parallel to the other, the one on the higher level lined with chestnut trees, and one day I saw, as I was walking along the lower path, Karen on the higher, walking at the same pace as I. I sat on a bench at the end of the park, just inside the gate, where the two paths converged. When Karen approached me, I moved to the side. She sat by me.

"Hi," she said.

"Hi," I answered.

Though I was near one end of the bench, I moved farther toward the end.

"I've got an orange," she said. "Would you like some?"

She placed a book across her knees and from a pocket of her raincoat took an orange, which she placed on the book and peeled. She split the peeled orange into sections, gave me one, and ate one herself.

Chewing, I said, "Thanks."

The scar stood out on her lower lip when she smiled.

"I went to a lecture," she said.

"I'm glad."

"I didn't make much of it, though. I'm afraid the scholastic year is for me *raté*."

"Nothing is ever *raté*. You can make up past lectures."

"How?"

"I can try to help you."

"It's cold here," she said. "I think we should walk a little."

We walked down by the breweries. In a row of low stone houses I saw a café. The Flemish workers sat still when I, who had learned the Flemish manner of going into a public place before the woman with me, went into the grim café. Karen followed me to a wooden table. We sat for a while in the stillness before the proprietor came over and, his large forearms bare, grabbed the edge of the table and leaned forward and said, in awkward French, that the *étudiants* had their own cafés, and this was not one of them. I smiled up at him and calmly ordered beer, *frites,* herrings in brine and onions, and bread, and the proprietor said, "Very well."

As Karen and I ate and drank, she said, "Look at that," indicating with a nod of her head an old man in wooden clogs, his heavy, gaunt hand resting on the table, a blue cloth tied about his neck, a big framed mirror on the wall behind him. "Look," she kept saying, nodding and glancing about. She was doing this for me, I knew, was insisting on staying in a place where we were not welcome because everything there was an object of attention, and she wanted me to know she was attentive.

When we walked around the town, Karen pointed out to me statues in odd corners.

We did a lot together, Karen and I, that we wouldn't have done separately. Using a guide I'd bought to take her to places we didn't already know, we saw, outside the town, an old abbey with a grass-covered courtyard and brick buildings and a church.

On a weekend, we drove around the Ardennes to see the countryside. Karen had wanted to do this — the first time she proposed an excursion. For lunch we bought pâté from the *charcuterie* on the main street of a village, a long loaf of bread from the bakery, and apples from a grocery, and took these off to the forest to eat. Because of the damp, we ate in the car, parked in a clearing to the side of a dirt road. Then we walked along the paths through the trees, still winter bare but as if swelling with the humidity in the air; the branches were wet and dripped. We studied a fallen tree covered with moss and flat, semicircular wood mushrooms that grew through the moss.

Among the rotting leaves at our feet I spotted a sheet of stained paper with writing, and I picked it up: an old letter, the script, in blue ink, so diffused by damp that we could only read a few words, such as *beaucoup* and *oui* and *notre*. As she tried to read it, tears filled Karen's eyes.

The day before Vincent was to get out of the hospital, Karen and I went, she as usual driving the rented car, to Gonesse to spend the night in a hotel and bring him back to Louvain in the morning.

It was raining when we arrived in Gonesse. With nothing to do, we visited the municipal museum, a small, run-down château with creaky wooden floors, and pointed out to each other, in glass cases, reliquaries, carved ivories, rings, medallions, embroidery in gold and silver thread.

Karen said, "That's beautiful."

"Extraordinary."

"Wonderful," she said. "Wonderful."

Again I knew she was doing this for me. She turned to me and smiled, and I, my eyes searching hers, smiled back.

That evening, we sat alone in the chilly dining room of the hotel after the few other guests had left and drank cognac.

As if she had been waiting for the moment, Karen said, startling me, "Tom's mother and I have been writing to each other."

"His mother —"

"She said that she and Tom's father asked to have the lid of the coffin he was transported in lifted. They didn't recognize him."

"Why?"

Karen shook her head.

"She said they would like to know about Tom's life here, what he did every day, what he said, who his friends were. I wrote that you were Tom's closest friend. She said she knew about you from his letters. She'd appreciate hearing from you. Will you write to her?"

In the morning, the sky was clear. Vincent paused along the gravel from the hospital to the car to look up at the flying gulls.

I sent a letter to Tom's parents and had one back from his mother in which she wrote they were happy that I was alive.